TERROR TRAILS

Books by Barry Smith

The Kimberley Trilogy
For Freedom's Cause
Battle for the North
Kimberley Kill

Victoria's Twins —
The Rise of Manchester and Melbourne

Terror Trails

TERROR TRAILS

BARRY SMITH

DEDICATION

Ken Siddons

With thanks to and in loving memory of Ken Siddons, my Manchester boyhood mentor and dear friend.

Inspirational Australian Writers

Neville Shute, Arthur Upfield, Peter Temple and **Peter Corris** have entertained and inspired me to try my hand in this action/adventure genre with an Australian edge.

Miquel and **Riitta,** who helped me with the Spanish and Finnish, settings.

ACKNOWLEDGEMENTS

My grateful thanks to:

Rev George and **Jane Markotsis** who invited me to escape the southern winter by minding their new Brisbane home, where much of this novel was imagined and written.

Helen Bradfield Croll, who audited forensically, from an authentic Australian, reader's perspective and spoke up for Kat's interests, mirroring her passions and feminine wiles.

Sandra Bailey, who wielded her teacher's red pen ruthlessly and determinedly asked common-sense questions of a far from common-sense writer.

Coral Brown, who threw the odd critical hand grenade to ensure good taste and literary convention were addressed.

Ian Dick and **Suzanne Blair**, who contributed advice about representational and promotional issues.

The Yeronga Park Deep Water Running Group, who made me welcome and enabled me to come back down from literary dreaming, whilst pretending to get as fit as them.

CONTENTS

HISTORICAL NOTE

(Thanks to Manchester Evening News)

On June 15, 1996, the IRA singled out Manchester to be victim of the biggest bomb it had ever exploded on the British mainland. It would injure hundreds and leave no building within half a mile unscathed. This was a blast that tore through the heart of Manchester and which, within seconds, would have an impact that would last for two decades.

Just a few months earlier the Provos had ended a 17-month ceasefire by blowing up a lorry in Canary Wharf, killing two people. In Manchester things were more relaxed. But police were nonetheless prepared for trouble — as thousands of football fans poured into town ahead of that afternoon's Euro 96 match between England and Scotland.

Unknown and unnoticed, a white van was already on its devastating journey. Just before 9.20 am, the streets had already begun filling up with crowds when two men in hooded anoraks and sunglasses left a heavily loaded Ford Cargo van outside Marks and Spencer on the corner of Cannon Street and Corporation Street. It was parked on double yellow lines with its hazard lights flashing. It contained 3,300 pounds of homemade explosive, three times the size of the Canary Wharf bomb.

They walked away, ringing an IRA chief in Ireland to let them know the job was done. The pair escaped in a burgundy Ford Granada, later abandoned in Preston. Three minutes after the van was abandoned, a traffic warden slapped a ticket on it.

Sometime after 9.38 am a man with an Irish accent called Granada TV, Sky News, Salford University, North Manchester General Hospital and the Garda police in Dublin to warn a bomb would go off in one hour. He gave the location and used a code word known to Special Branch.

On their CCTV camera in Bootle Street station, officers watched in horror as footage was relayed showing people pushing up against and sliding along the side of the van, awkwardly parked on one of the city's busiest shopping streets.

Officers then began one of the most extraordinary policing operations the country has ever seen: the evacuation of 80,000 people.

At first, they were not keen to go. Mancunians had become used to bomb scares and they had things to be getting on with. One hairdresser refused to let his clients leave because they still had chemicals in their hair, arguing it would be 'too dangerous'. A group of workmen wanted to stay put because they were on weekend rates. Police officer Wendy McCormick found herself telling people in the Arndale: "I don't want to die because somebody won't finish their pizza."

It was a Herculean task, aided by the luck of having extra police on duty for the match. Gradually, grudgingly, people began to move, turning into a flood as word spread that the scare was real. The police cordon extended out and out to a quarter of a mile, until there were no more officers to take it any further.

By 11.10 am, the heart of Manchester city centre was deserted. Only one or two people were still within the exclusion zone, having somehow escaped knowledge of the evacuation. A pair of women working in the Arndale, on their way out for a walk, were only saved because they nipped back inside to get their bags. Two minutes before the blast, they were standing on the bridge directly above it.

Shortly after 11 am the army bomb disposal squad — which had hurtled to Manchester down the M62 from Liverpool — was preparing to detonate the device from 200 yards away, just off Cross Street near Sam's Chophouse.

When the bomb exploded, the blast could be heard from 15 miles away. It issued a force so powerful it travelled around 90 degree corners, knocking people to the ground and blowing out virtually every window within half a mile, leaving a 15 metre crater around it.

Glass rained from the sky: a fine dust followed by shards and eventually a torrent of rubble and debris. From his vantage point on Cross Street, Chief Inspector Ian Seabridge later recalled that there was then a 'sudden air of stillness'.

Then every alarm in the city centre started wailing.

More than 200 people were hurt in the blast. Yet one fact from that day remains breathtaking — and a testament to that heroic policing operation. Nobody had been killed. Nevertheless, Manchester city centre lay in ruins. Mannequins hung eerily from windows. Historic landmarks such as Manchester Cathedral, Chetham's School of Music, the Corn Exchange and the Royal Exchange theatre would take years and millions of pounds to restore. Strangely, one of the features that survived unscathed was a red post box from Queen Victoria's reign.

Much of the city centre became a no-go zone for its residents and shopkeepers. Some 700 businesses were affected, wiping out a third of the city centre's floor-space and leaving the council to leap into action in the days that followed in an attempt to save livelihoods.

The bomb would be only the start of a much longer story.

ABBREVIATIONS

ASIO — Australian Secret Intelligence Organisation
ASIS — Australian Secret Intelligence Service
ASIS and ASIO have in common the fact they both collect intelligence from human sources but there are substantial differences between the two agencies. ASIS's work relates to foreign intelligence.

ASIO's role is limited only by its function of security intelligence not by geography. Another important difference is that while human intelligence constitutes the majority of ASIS's work, ASIO's human collection is only one part of its work as an integrated collection, assessment and advisory agency.

C — Control, head of MI6
Its first director was Captain Sir Mansfield George Smith-Cumming, who often dropped the *Smith* in routine communication. He typically signed correspondence with his initial C in green ink. This usage evolved as a code name, and has been adhered to by all subsequent directors of SIS when signing documents to retain anonymity.

DG — Director General, head of MI5

FSB — Foreign Service Bureau (*Federalnaya Sluzhba Bezopasnosti*)
Federal Security Service (FSB). Russian internal security

and counter intelligence service created in 1994 as one of the successor agencies to the Soviet-era KGB.

GCHQ — Government Communications Head Quarters
The British Government's electronic intelligence gathering agency, principally located in Cheltenham, UK. This is the contemporary successor to the WW2 code breaking establishment at Bletchley Park.

MI6 — Military Intelligence, section 6
The Secret Intelligence Service (SIS), commonly known as MI6, is the foreign intelligence service of the government of the United Kingdom, tasked mainly with the covert overseas collection and analysis of human intelligence (HUMINT) in support of the UK's national security. SIS is a member of the country's intelligence community and its Chief is accountable to the country's Foreign Secretary.

The stated priority roles of SIS are counter-terrorism, counter-proliferation, providing intelligence in support of cyber security, and supporting stability overseas to disrupt terrorism and other criminal activities.

MI5 — Military Intelligence, section 5
The Security Service, also MI5, is the United Kingdom's domestic counter-intelligence and security agency and is part of its intelligence machinery alongside the Secret Intelligence Service.

MOSSAD — Israeli intelligence agency

NHS — National Health Service

SAS — Special Air Service
The Special Air Service (SAS) is a Special Forces unit

of the British Army. The SAS was founded in 1941 as a regiment, and later reconstituted as a corps in 1950. The unit undertakes a number of roles including covert reconnaissance, counter-terrorism, direct action and hostage rescue.

SBS — Special Boat Service
The Special Boat Service (SBS) is the Special Forces unit of the Royal Navy of the United Kingdom. The SBS can trace its origins to the Second World War to the Army Special Boat Section formed in 1940.

UMIST — University of Manchester Institute of Science and Technology.

UNCOMMON WORD GLOSSARY

Potcheen — Highly alcoholic Irish spirit which used to be made, illegally, using home-made stills.
Slutch — Northern English description of black slime.
Snag — Australian slang for a Sausage
Strine — Australian dialect.
Wuss — A wimp. A Feeble person.
Naughty — Australian slang for sexual intercourse.

1
THE BOMB

Her responsive tremor lured his fingers downward, from cupping her pert breasts, to twining tendrils of her lush, pubic thatch, when the bomb went off. The flash penetrated the bedroom blinds, the bed vibrated and then came the deafening bang.

"Christ almighty! What was that?" she shrieked, leaping out of bed, without bothering to conceal her ivory nakedness.

"I don't know. A big explosion and not too far from here I think. There are no chemical storages in the city. Could be a gas leak, but it was so loud I fear it might have been a bomb."

Seeing her so shaken and tearful, he jumped up, grabbed a blanket and wrapped her in his warm, reassuring embrace.

"Don't worry love, it was not close enough to hurt us, you are quite safe here, but God help any poor buggers nearby."

An unnatural silence followed, as though all of Manchester had shut down.

But this was soon shattered by the siren-wails of

emergency units and the roar of heavy vehicles racing to the scene.

Ken drew the blind and opened the window. It was nearly noon on a grey and lowering day. From his third floor apartment in the market complex of the Northern Quarter, the towering clouds of black smoke were directly in his line of sight.

"It's somewhere down near the Cathedral. I can see the smoke. But it's not exactly clear where the centre of the explosion is."

When she assured him that she was alright to go, she left to return to the safety of her home in the northern suburbs and Ken rang his fire officer, brother, to find out what had happened.

"Not much I can tell you Ken excepting that we had forty-five minutes warning that an IRA bomb would go off in the retail centre. So far there's no news of casualties or damage. All I can reassure you about is that your favourite Shambles pub complex has survived."

Ken began to feel the after effects of this shocking incident and what came foremost to his mind was the memory of his mother gathering him and his brother behind a curtain, under the stairs, whenever a thunder storm passed — fearful as ever as a result of her living through the wartime Manchester blitz.

TV news was on the job and all manner of lurid stories dominated the reports — much about nothing as usual, and all falling short when it came to the facts about what had happened. Ken realised there was no point in going out and trying to visit the site, so he followed his usual routine, after a very fulfilling bout of love making, by putting on an espresso pot of Blue Mountain coffee and running a hot bath, infused with scented, spicy oils.

The coffee and the relaxing warmth of the bath almost lulled him to sleep but then his insatiable curiosity kicked in. Who had done this and why? For Ken, this was not the idle curiosity of a general member of the public. It was only five years since he had returned from Australia, the survivor of a terrorist assassination attempt and with the commendation and collusion of the Australian Security Intelligence Organisation. This atrocity could have nothing to do with his former life at the bottom of the world but, nonetheless, a frisson of fear ran through him.

The persistent ringing of his phone broke through his reverie and drew him out of the comforting warmth of the scented waters, to answer the call.

2
BACK IN THE GAME

Manchester, Sam's Chop House

The smoke from the fires had penetrated every layer of his clothing and its sooty, pall lurked in his lungs. Blowing into a tissue to clear his sinuses, he was reminded of delivering Christmas mail in the sixties through impenetrable chemical smog, which left a rime of slutch on the scarf covering his mouth. Then the waiter arrived with their orders.

"Here we are gents, steak and kidney pudding for you sir and for your friend our famous corned beef hash and two pints of Guinness. That will put lead in your pencils."

The traditional Lancastrian fare and the historical setting were most comforting to Ken, but when he looked into the eyes of the man opposite him, a fearful unease gripped his bowels. There was nothing to suggest that Harry Higgins was anyone special, let alone dangerous, but as MI5's anti-terrorist officer in the north his success in penetrating agents' cells and eradicating their members by all means both legal and expedient, was legendary.

"Sorry to butt back into your life again Ken, especially after the rough time you had down under. But from what you have just seen of the IRA's handiwork — the retail centre of Manchester destroyed and several hundred people injured — we need all the help we can call upon to ensure this doesn't happen again."

"I am horrified by what I saw today — a whole street destroyed and only the post box from Queen Victoria's era left unscathed. It must have been a hell of a bomb."

"Fifteen hundred kilograms of high explosive and, but for the coded warning, thousands would have died."

"Sickening that so-called Christian people could stoop so low in pursuit of a political cause. I am disgusted, but I am still unsure why I am sitting here with you. I was assured that I would be allowed to live a normal life here and, if necessary, under your protection from eastern bloc assassins. Despite my experience in Australia I am still not a trained agent and have no connection whatsoever with the Irish community neither here nor there. So what am I doing having lunch with you?"

"Before I answer you Ken, I need to remind you that you were required to sign the Official Secrets Act as part of your settlement back here, because what I am about to share with you is top secret. Do you understand and agree to remain true to your commitment?"

"As far as keeping what you are about to tell me secret, I agree."

"Good. Just relax and let me order you another Guinness, before I fill you in on the background to our problems here. I need not go over the menace of IRA hit squads and their deadly bombing campaign in Northern Ireland and on the British mainland. But let me assure you that our interest in bringing you back into the fold has nothing directly to do with the IRA, nor the Irish.

You see, the Irish terrorist cause is compromised by our infiltration of their organisation up to the highest levels and though they can still maim and kill, they will never win what they want by such violence, so long as we are prepared to accept the limited loss of life and wait until public opinion in Ireland has had enough of endless maiming and killing. Our concern is with the wider threat of terrorism and especially, arms smuggling connected with the Jugoslav civil war, the rogue Iranian regime and disgruntled Argentinian elements who have not accepted the outcome of the Falklands war. Behind all this lurks the hand of the Russians still smarting at the collapse of their Soviet Empire."

"Yes, very instructive and not news to me, apart from the IRA hierarchy being penetrated, but I still cannot see how I can help you."

"Manchester is a hotbed of these arms and munitions trades and we need a better understanding of who is dealing in what and where. You are an inconspicuous Manchester man but with the experience of winning the trust of Croatian communities in Australia resulting in the prevention of terrorist plots. We want you to do the same thing here but the greater difficulty is that we need to cast our enquiry net wider than over any one community or grouping."

"I understand the necessity of your needs and I deplore the loss of innocent civilian lives but I really don't feel up to this task."

"Ken, remember: they tried to kill the Prime Minister and cabinet; they laid siege to the Iranian embassy; terrorists brought off the Lockerbie aircraft bombing; they killed two people in their previous Manchester bombing; and in Warrington they killed children as well as adults. We need to break the supply of weapons and sophisticated explosives to these zealots."

"Your argument is compelling, but if I agree, how can you make me more capable of pulling this off?"

"We are not seeking a 007 operative. It is your very innocuous, ordinariness that is your main value to us and your ability to blend into the Manchester environment. But having said that, we will send you to one of our special training centres to augment your skills and especially to improve your survivability."

3
SCHOOL FOR SPIES

Derbyshire Dales

The drive through the Derbyshire Dales, in a top of the line Range Rover, was swift and smooth until its sudden turn off the bitumen onto a bumpy, dirt track led through a succession of narrow gorges to an electrified security fence. Their pace slowed momentarily, whilst a remotely controlled gate admitted them to the well-manicured parkland of a stately Georgian Mansion that proved to be their destination.

Ken hopped out of the car and was greeted at the top of the steps by a tall and imposing soldier in camouflage dress which bore only the insignia of his rank.

"Good morning Lieutenant. Can I assume this is the spy school?"

"Welcome to the Grange sir. You are in the right place and if you hurry along the corridor you will just have time to grab a sandwich and cup of tea before the fun starts. I must remind you that you will be joining a number of other conference attendees with whom you will be working, but who will remain strangers to you. It is vital for the security of your future work that all you know about each other is your names and briefest of backgrounds.

So, there must be no deep and meaningful questioning and you must absolutely refrain from the temptation of extracurricular dalliances with members of either sex."

The corridor was lined with huge portraits, presumably of the owner's ancestors, interspersed with Napoleonic era furniture and obligatory stag's head. This led to a spacious drawing room and the noisy babble of a crowd of tea-drinking fellow delegates. Whilst meat pies and sausage rolls were more to his taste, after his time in Australia, Ken was hungry enough to load his plate with crust-less cheese and cucumber sandwiches and at least one slice of veal and ham pie. The tea, on the other hand, was a more than acceptable Earl Grey.

Ever since his university days, he had been confounded by the best way to break into the tight squares of cocktail party cliques, and as far as he knew, there was no infallible stratagem for gaining their attention, short of dropping his trousers or spilling hot tea into the lap of the loudest bore. Fortunately the answer to this dilemma came in the delightful form of a slender, ash-blonde, who seemed equally aloof or excluded from the main throng.

"Hello! Are you as shy as me, or do you also hate such occasions?"

"G'day. The latter, I must admit, but it will not be long before the briefing session starts and there should be just enough time for you to put away that plate full of grub."

"Yes, well, it was a non-stop journey here and I have had no lunch."

"No need to justify yourself to me mate, if I weren't pretending to play the lady-like part, I would be wolfing down a plateful, though the fare is a bit bland for my taste."

"Can I assume that pies and sauce with the odd snag and dim-sim might be more your style."

"Very perceptive of you, and in return, can I assume your knowledge of Aussie cuisine was gathered down under, or are you a fan of Bazza McKenzie movies?"

For the brief interlude before the conference started and between sandwich bites, Ken became as acquainted as the rules allowed with Katherine — call me Kat — Douglas from Sydney and at least confirmed that when not putting on the Strine, her well-rounded vowels betrayed an expensive private school education with a free mind and spirit barely tamed by time served at an Antipodean university.

The opening address by a senior MI5 officer set the tone for the forthcoming programme. It was not intended that participants be converted from their normal civilian ways into mythical 007-style operatives. Whilst there would be some familiarisation with defensive techniques and weapons training, the main focus would be more on cerebral and interpersonal skills development. The selection of the venue bore this out. Although the rear entry and annex in which they would hold their sessions ensured privacy, the house was still the home of a leading aristocratic family and through its front entrance and beautiful, Capability Brown crafted grounds, public visitors were welcomed.

Ken found the month-long training in trade craft, and especially the sharpening of his listening and character assessment skills, interesting and stretching. Most difficult was the need to develop the impassivity required in adopting differing identities, to blend almost invisibly into social settings and to maintain his adopted role, when under suspicion and possibly brutal interrogation. Little did he appreciate how critical they would become to his success as an operative and even more so to his staying alive. He had heeded the warnings about over fraternisation with fellow trainees and despite spending little time working with her, he had still developed a liking for the sophisticated and smart Australian woman concealed beneath her dinky-di Aussie veneer. He was soon to find out much more about her and come to rely on her capabilities.

4
ON THE MUNITIONS TRAIL

Oldham

The Izmir was far from the best Turkish restaurant he had eaten in but its crowded clientele of local Muslims, inexpensive and earthy food met his needs, perfectly.

"How's your Yogurtlu kebab, Kat?"

"Interesting, but the combination of garlic and tomato sauce seems like an unfortunate collision of cultures."

"Perhaps it was an initiative of Ataturk when he was westernising the Turkish Republic. It's my favourite Turkish dish, when done properly, but this is not nearly as good as my first one in an Ankara restaurant in the seventies. Heinz sauce is no substitute for fresh tomato puree."

"Can you see our man?"

"Yes, he's the only other white person here, sitting at a table on his own, near the kitchen. Don't draw attention to him, he will make contact when he is ready and it's safe to do so."

The man wiped his mouth with his napkin and having paid his bill stood up to leave. As he passed their table he stooped to pick up a fallen paper napkin and placed it by Ken's plate and advised:

"If you like the food as much I do, you will need this to clear up after. Bon appetite."

After he had left, Ken unfolded the napkin and tucked it into the collarof his shirt, as a guard against errant drops of yogurt and tomato sauce. He was well known for eating with more gusto than delicacy.

"Time to be going Kat, or we will miss our appointment."

As soon as they had stepped out into the cool night air she asked Ken, "How will we know where to meet him?"

He wrote on the napkin: 'Meet me in ten in the Blue Lion up the street.'

Their contact was easy to spot. Although he had been out of the military for years, he was still in good shape, his casual dress was much neater than that of the usual Blue Lion denizens and he still polished his shoes. When standing, he was a tall, imposing figure and his handshake was proof of his fitness and strength.

"Pull up a pew and I'll get your drinks. What's your poison?"

"A pint of Guinness for me and a lemon, lime and bitters for Kat."

It was clear that he was a regular and valued patron, as the barman came over to take the order in person. He had chosen to meet them in a secluded settle that backed onto a wall, enabling them to talk freely without being overheard and to see anyone who might come close. When the drinks arrived Ken wasted no time in getting down to business.

"Before we start, why did you choose that hotbed of Islamists to arrange the meeting?"

"Simply because no self-respecting and probably Catholic, IRA man was likely to be eating there."

"We understand you might have something to tell us related to Manchester's problem the other day."

"I might if you are the people who can make proper use of it, to take out the bastards who blew up the town centre and keep my identity secure."

"We can give you that assurance as we represent an arm of government dedicated to fulfilling your wish. Before you say anything more, we would appreciate some evidence of your qualification for providing useful, information about this."

"Fair enough, but as far as who I am and where I come from, it's a case of name, rank and number only."

"That seems reasonable, so assure us that you are worth listening to."

"I was a professional member of her Majesty's forces until recently. As a former sapper with active service in the Falklands, Balkans and Northern Ireland, I know a thing or two about high explosives and their use in booby trapping premises and killing unsuspecting military and civilian enemies. Returning to civvy street is always a challenge for men like me and the severance pay by no means enables me to afford the style of life I became accustomed to when travelling abroad at government expense. Private contractors pay much better and I have worked for the best of them."

"So, you are a mercenary?"

"If you must use that term, I was, but more a highly specialised and well-rewarded contractor with some strong principles about whom I would work for, and who

I would fight against. Not all of my former colleagues had such scruples and so I am as much aware of the best as well as the cowboys for hire by the highest bidder. I have some idea of where supplies of explosives, such as Semtex and related armaments come from and how they get into the hands of irregulars and terrorists."

"So what do you have to tell us and why?"

"First of all, why? I have done and seen some terrible things in the course of my duties but nothing as barbaric as these Irish cunts have done in killing innocent ex-service men and families at a war memorial ceremony, drinkers in a packed Birmingham pub and now the destruction of the retail heart of my city. At least there was some warning and nobody was killed this time, but hundreds were injured and the damage and deprivation of services will take years to repair and replace. As for the what, whilst I have no detailed information about who carries out these atrocities, I can point you in the direction of those who are supplying them the necessary munitions and weapons."

"We would appreciate hearing anything you can tell us about that. But I must stress that we are not authorised to offer any payment."

"Although I have been a mercenary, I am still a patriot, husband and father, and I cannot turn a blind eye to the doings of these evil men and I expect no payment for contributing to their eradication. When you have seen the terrible evidence of the torture and execution of young squaddies, who were naïve enough to fall victim to the allures of pretty young, Irish republican tarts, the desire for retribution becomes very personal."

"OK, what have you got for us?"

"It's common knowledge that Semtex comes originally from the manufacturers in Czechoslovakia and that the small arms also come from various countries behind the former iron curtain. But what's less clear are the channels through which they flow to the end users. Most terrorist supplies come from either Iran or Gaddafi's regime, in Libya and in the case of the IRA, the route into Europe starts in Spain. Once across the Spanish border the EU's open borders facilitate onward transport to Ireland, and of course some stays with ETA, the Basque terror group, who are happy to collaborate with their Irish counterparts. So I recommend that you go trawling for more information in Barcelona or Madrid, where, as well as plenty of expat Brits, many of dubious reputation, there are clusters of Irish and Middle Eastern natives who are happy to do business with each other that leads to outrages in western countries.

Spanish external security was slack under Franco but with ETA on the rampage and what they learned from protecting the Barcelona Olympic Games, I am sure they would be happy to cooperate with any MI6 operation which reduced their terrorist exposure. I have no specific information about who is involved and where they are located but I am sure that the Spanish authorities are well aware of underworld haunts and perhaps the hangouts of Russian and Balkan mafia interests who operate strictly within the limits of the law.

There are so many Brits there you could easily enter in the guise of tourists or people seeking to buy a home for holidays and retirement, but be aware, if you are identified as spying on their activities, your end will be certain, slow and cruelly painful, especially for women agents. That's all I have to tell you, except to add that anyone following this trail is much braver than me. Now, I will bid you good night and slip back into the anonymity of my regular non-military life."

"Well, that was lighter on detail than I had hoped for, but it is a start and at least narrows down our search to at least one European country for starters."

"I agree Ken, and if we follow his advice we will have to take extreme caution in preparing our bona fides before poking around in the Spanish underworld's lairs."

"Let's finish our drinks and get back to base to report on what we have learned. Any decision as to whether to follow up on this lead and who might take it on is out of our hands."

5
IN PLAIN SIGHT

London, MI5 HQ

The news of the Spanish link came as no surprise to the MI5 hierarchy, but the tip off — from Oldham at least — confirmed suspicions and gave credence to the proposal that an operation to make further enquiries in Spain was justified. The British government had reason to be wary of the security of information shared via the EU bureaucracy and so it was deemed safer to make overtures to Spain through proven and trusted back channels.

The contribution of British volunteers to the republican cause during the Spanish Civil War was still appreciated by certain members of the post-Franco Spanish government. During World War II, relations between the Royal and Spanish navies were cordial, despite Spain's neutrality and certainly less hostile than those with Franco and his army. The visit of a Spanish frigate to London, therefore, provided an excellent opportunity for an informal meeting between members of each nation's naval intelligence services at the dinner, held in the Royal Naval College's painted hall, at Greenwich, in honour of the arrival of this less invasive Armada.

London, Private club

The informality and deniability of the meeting between the heads of MI5, MI6 and Naval Intelligence was evidenced by its being held at the Foreign Secretary's club. She opened by confirming that the proposed penetration into Spain was approved by the Prime Minister and had the endorsement of the Spanish Prime Minister. She stressed that knowledge of this decision was confined to these leaders and those meeting with her in the club's library.

"We consider this opportunity to clearly identify the source and pathway of illegal arms and munitions shipments into Spain, and on to anti-British terror groups, of vital importance. But as the area of interest is within the EU we need to keep it sufficiently under wraps that it does not get caught up in the Union's complex decision processes and become common knowledge to all member countries' security forces and thereby risking a leak about its existence falling into the wrong hands."

"Thank you, Minister, for supporting our plan to insert agents into Spain. We at Naval Intelligence agree with our Spanish counterparts that to send regular British agents would risk their being identified and I would like you to hear from Control at MI6 how we propose to minimise this risk and at least make it readily deniable."

"You may recall ma'am, that a joint citizen of the UK and Australia returned home to Manchester, after helping to unmask and thwart Jugoslav Intelligence operations aimed at causing unrest in Australia's migrant communities. We have kept a watching brief on him to ensure that he has not attracted the attention of eastern bloc intelligence agencies and that he has kept out of trouble. MI5 reports that he has settled back into his community and is very much an unremarkable citizen of Manchester. As a result of the IRA outrage there, he was approached and asked whether he might help us with information gathering, much as he did in Australia amongst the Croat community. We considered that his experience in this limited role and commonplace, appearance could be of real value.

As a result of his initiative we confirmed the Spanish link and we suggest that he is the right person to go into Spain under the cover of yet another Brit seeking time in the sun. He would be accompanied by a female agent, posing as his wife or girlfriend, who likewise, is newly recruited with no previous, traceable field exposure. In effect, they would be hiding in plain sight."

"There is obvious risk in sending green agents but I understand your logic and I suppose in the event of their getting into trouble it would be easier to protest that they are innocent and naïve British holiday makers, whose curiosity got the better of them."

"That's true ma'am and in the worst possible eventuality we could rely on our Spanish colleagues to arrest them on some trumped up charge and after a brief incarceration, deport them back to us."

"Very well, I will defer to your professional judgement and you are free to go ahead, but there will be nothing in writing and we will not support you publicly if things go awry."

"Thank you, ma'am. We will proceed as planned."

"Keep me informed and good luck."

6
A SPANISH HOLIDAY

On the night train

On the night sleeper train from Paris to Madrid, Ken and Kat had plenty of time to reflect upon the challenge ahead of them, to get to know each other better, and to perfect the story about their relationship and reason for visiting Spain out of summer season.

Neither would pass as visiting historians, their Spanish was poor and tourists are less likely to visit Madrid in February, but an ingenious form of cover had been proposed by their Spanish contact. They were signed up as external expatriate faculty on an English conversation course for Spanish professionals, which required no expertise other than that they were able to spend a week in a comfortable out of town resort hotel, conversing with Spanish professionals in English. Also, their unusual entry to Madrid, by train, made their arrival even less noticeable than if they had come directly by plane.

As the train rocked into the night, passing through southern France, Ken and Kat learned more about each other.

"Why did you get into this game Kat?"

"More by design than you, I believe. I come from a

military family in Australia which has always been pro-British, devoted to the monarchy, and it was through my father, who is a retired General that I came to the attention of MI5."

"Sounds rather contrived and passive on your part."

"Not so. I hold strong views about global politics and I am alarmed at the way you British sleep-walked into an undemocratic EU, surrendering your hard won libertarian birthright, whilst Russia and China grow in influence unchecked other than by the Yanks. So I decided I would like to do my bit towards rebalancing the scales."

"Australians answering the Empire's call again, eh?"

"You're a cynical bastard. Being stood up by Britain in favour of the EU turned out to be a blessing in disguise. We have never been so self-reliant and confident of our place in the world and of our ability to thrive as a democratic island in an Asian sea. Despite immigration restrictions, young Australians still help to keep London and the NHS running. So we have not given up on you, yet."

"You have to be sceptical in this job where politicians are our masters."

"So what drives you?

"Whilst I subscribe to your view of how the world is shaping up, I'm more driven by personal concerns. Great injustices by the state in Australia against a Croat minority made me get into this game, and the bombing of the heart of my home city made me really mad and determined to put a spoke in any terrorist's wheel."

"I guess we are broadly in agreement, even if we come at it from different starting points. So, how are we going to play this so-called holiday in Spain?"

"For me it will be easy, just playing my real inquisitive, disarming self — the quintessential Brit abroad, wanting ever so helpfully to impart to the Spaniards the superiority of our language and culture."

"Aren't you the raw prawn?"

"That's what I need to be, and you, the typical whinging Aussie telling everyone how much better it is there, whilst half your nation is elsewhere, oohing and awing at the delights of other cultures. You will be an independent girlfriend seeming ready to leave me at the drop of a hat, who argues with me a lot, but who seeks assurance and protection from me when things get sticky. Think you can do that?"

"It'll be a stretch, mate, especially the weak and clinging maiden bit, but your style will make it easy to be bolshie."

"Good, better get our heads down, we will be in Madrid in a few hours."

7
LOOSE LIPS

Belfast bar

"Seamus, did we get anything out of that blabber-mouthed soldier boy?"

"Not much. We squeezed him hard and he will never walk again, but all he would admit to was some loose-mouthed boasting about his army service to a couple in an Oldham pub. Even when we nailed him to the floor through his knees he kept to this story, and so they are either innocent, or he is a very brave man.

The barman is one of ours and he confirmed that the couple looked ordinary and harmless, especially the gormless fella, and the woman is Australian. They couldn't be members of British intelligence."

"Have you followed up with our London boys?"

"Aye, we sent them a description of the pair and nobody made them as agents or Special Branch members known to us. Seems the guy spent some time in Australia and so, not so surprisingly, he has an Aussie sheila in tow. He's what they call a Human Resources Manager, in a large company, very low key, ordinary, and pretty popular with the workers according to our union man in there."

"Ok, no harm done, but at least it will send out a warning to others who endanger us by blabbing in pubs. Now, how are the arms plans going?"

"Gaddafi's people are prepared to let us have all the Semtex we need. As well as the usual supply of Kalashnikovs, they have some very neat shoulder launched missiles too, that could be useful for downing army helicopters and perhaps an airliner at Heathrow."

"What about getting them here undetected?"

"We have a shared deal with ETA, and with their help and bribery of customs officials and police, we can get an assignment into the Spanish enclave of Ceuta on the tip of Morocco, which is a hop step and a jump from the Spanish mainland. Once on European soil, the open borders policy makes it easy to truck it all the way to a port across from Britain and ship it directly into dear old Eire, where, as you know, we have bought blind eyes and deaf ears a plenty."

"Good work, but what about the funds to pay for this. How is that progressing?"

"Gaddafi was going to use some of the mining union's money that they sent him for safe keeping, well beyond Maggie's clutches, during their strike.

But we thought that was in danger of drawing the deal to the attention of British intelligence and so we have turned to other sources."

"What are they?"

"The usual KGB paymasters. It will come from St Petersburg, but I am not sure how. The Yanks and Brits watch international money movements like hawks, but it seems there is an untraceable Islamic method of transferring money that has been used by the faithful over centuries."

"Keep your eye on that, and let me know when it is all coming together so that I can start to grease the wheels of our influential allies here in Ireland and London. Soon we will have enough explosive power to make Manchester seem like Guy Fawkes' night."

8
FRIENDS IN NEED

Madrid, in winter

The Madrid metro was much smarter and more modern than the Tube. Even so the carriages were equally packed. Somehow, every week seemed to be a festive occasion there, and true to form groups of musicians played their way through the train. The small, lively combo were equally at home playing gypsy music and jazz, and at sight of Ken and Kat broke into a spirited rendition of *Hit the road Jack ...* all good fun and sure to bring a smile to passengers, but Ken was aware of pick pocketing and other thieving techniques carried out by Eastern European and South American crime gangs, as well as desperate, jobless Spaniards. He and Kat secured their bags behind them to ensure the performers could not surround and distract them, allowing accomplices to steal their luggage. Then to add to the hilarity, Roman legionaries, in full armour, came aboard collecting for a charity — probably anti-thief police in disguise. Welcome to modern Madrid.

The Puerta del Sol was crowded with shoppers, demonstrators, African refugees selling tat, gawping tourists, frozen statue artists, and a few bored Municipal

Police. The Petit Palace Hotel is strategically placed at the junction of pedestrian streets running down from the square, and offers an unobtrusive façade with a low cost, comfortable, tourist package and friendly service. Just the sort of place travellers on a tight budget would pick.

They filled in the time before they were due at the briefing session for the conversation workshop, strolling along the lanes, through squares and sitting in café windows enjoying people watching and glasses of rich, ruby red, Rioja.

The briefing took the form of a tapas and drinks party, and those present were expatriate English speakers from all around the world. There was the usual mix of perpetual conference attenders: odd men and women; Brits, some of whose accents were a mystery to Ken, surely an impossible challenge for the Spanish; ubiquitous Antipodeans and both loudly brash and quiet, sophisticated, Americans. They were invited to join a bus, early in the morning which would take them to their resort conference — hotel in the snow-capped Gredos Mountains, three hours out of Madrid.

The twelve hour contact days required intense one-on-one conversations with, and intent listening to, delightful, smart, Spanish professionals from a variety of occupational disciplines and different parts of Spain who, already, spoke good English. In the evenings, after a nine o'clock dinner, cultural activities, skits and charades, all in English, led to informal chatting in the bar, allowing the young and the foolhardy to rave into the small hours.

Ken's Anglo scorn of the siesta soon evaporated when he lowered his aching body and tired mind into a super warm sudsy spa bath, from which he could look out across the surrounding snow-coated fields. As boyfriend and girlfriend, Ken and Kat shared a room and separate beds. But their foresight in packing pyjamas and bathers avoided too much awkwardness and enabled them to share the spa.

"What do you make of it Ken?"

"What a brilliant idea. The Spaniards are super — where did the priest and black widow-ridden ones go? The food and wine are good and it truly is as promised, a four star hotel. I am going to enjoy this week."

"Yes, under other circumstances, I would readily volunteer for this experience, but I am always alert to the approach by our Spanish contact."

The connection, when it came, was deft and unobtrusive. Miquel, a former adviser to the Catalan provincial government, and now, as his party was out of power, a manager in an IT company, was Ken's favourite conversational partner. During the course of their second session, he revealed his hand.

"Ken, you have asked me about Catalan independence aspirations and ETA violence but how do you feel about your IRA?"

"Especially after the explosion in my home city which, whilst it killed nobody, ripped the heart out of the central retail area and injuredseveral hundred, I have nurtured an intense hatred of those wicked killers and I would welcome any act of revenge against them."

"What do you think could thwart their evil activities?"

"Armed resistance can only do so much and has caused loss of military lives similar to our annual road toll, but if a way could be found to starve them of money and arms, their desperation would make them take risks that might expose them to capture, and ultimately extinction."

"We have some experience here of trying to contain ETA, and if you wish, I would be pleased to discuss this with you, away from this formal environment and too many inquisitive ears."

"I would be very interested."

"Tonight we are due to go down to the village bar where they will be televising Real Madrid playing in a European cup match. With most people intent on the screen, and so noisy that it will be impossible for anyone to hear our conversation, this would be a natural and safe place for us to talk. Even though Franco is long gone, old habits of informing on friends and neighbours die hard, so we must be extra careful about how we meet and what we say."

"That sounds perfect and I will bring my girlfriend to make it more of an innocent looking social get together."

9
SECOND THOUGHTS

London, MI6 HQ

"Are we doing the right thing by Eliot and the Australian girl, C?"

"In what respect DG?"

"They are fairly lightly trained and probably don't realise how dangerous this assignment could be if they are exposed, and especially if captured by our enemies. I have been reading the report about that army Johnny's torture and looking at the pictures. Apart from the destruction of his face and burns all over his lower abdomen, they shot him through both elbows and nailed him to the floor through both his knees. He will never be the same man again. I am not so concerned about Eliot, as he ran the gauntlet successfully between Croats and Serb agents in Australia, and they are as bad if not worse than the IRA when it comes to interrogation and torture. But I am especially worried about the young lady."

"We were pretty specific about the risks associated with being blown. We could not have risked more established agents being made and we agreed that the very strength, and likely success of our fielding this so ordinary and green pair, was their ability to hide in plain sight. Douglas has no prior record to give her away, and unless Eliot runs into a former Croat associate or Serb agent he came up against in Australia, he will be equally free of scrutiny. It helps further that those parties do not operate outside the Balkans, without official direction from us or the Soviets, in respect of the Serbs, and if they were we would soon know about it. The Spaniards are not always forthcoming with information and appear to be lax, but whenever there is a threat of foreign incursion into their country they are wide awake and as equally effective as we would be in keeping tabs on them. That's why we have given them a heads-up on our activities in their back yard. But I can see that you are worried and there could be serious repercussions if some future enquiry under the full glare of the media found that we had sent lambs to their slaughter without thoroughly warning them and still having them volunteer.

How about I get a message to Eliot, really laying on the line the certainty of gruesome torture and a nasty death for both of them if they are detected? I could even include the graphic evidence of their informant's fate."

"Thank you C. I think it is the least we can do and I feel particularly responsible as my people selected, inducted and instructed them."

10
GET US THE MONEY

St Petersburg, Former KGB HQ

"Good morning comrade."

"Good morning comrade General. To what do I owe the pleasure of this invitation to your well-appointed office?"

"We only have what is necessary to serve the state and it is to further that I need your support. That clown Yeltsin is continuing the destruction of the Soviet Empire, that Gorbachev started, and if we can't do something to destabilise the west, it is the end of the KGB and you oligarchs, who are benefiting from the fire sale of our great state industries."

"I thought the KGB had been closed down."

"Almost, but a few of its loyal officers and some high ranking military patriots are preparing to restore the power we used to enjoy. We are able to do this, thanks to support from money-men, like you, who feel the same way."

"Tell me what we can do."

"You are aware of the IRA's successful bombing campaign and their recent success in destroying the heart of Manchester. This has seriously undermined the morale of the British public and builds on the disruption of their car production and the mining and power strikes of the eighties, which we sponsored through their militant unions. It has seriously wounded their economy and shaken their confidence in their government's ability to protect and feed them. The iron lady rallied them, but now they have turned on her and ended her Prime Ministership, they are very vulnerable and a stepped-up terrorist campaign might just break them."

"But they are part of the European Union. Surely they will be protected by the other members?"

"On the contrary, they opted out of the Maastricht treaty and will not join the proposed Monetary Union. They are not trusted and will not be supported against us. In any event they can do nothing without the military backing of the Americans. They don't even have the heavy lift aircraft to deploy their battle tanks against us without American air support. Apart from Britain, only the unpredictable French have a nuclear deterrent, and the Germans are reliant on our gas, especially in their harsh winters. Now the Serbs are resisting the break-up of Jugoslavia we are doing all we can to provoke conflict between them, Bosnia and Croatia and the Muslim minorities. This will keep the UN and Americans busy for the next few years. Now is the ideal time to provoke unrest in Britain and bring about a Socialist republic sympathetic to us."

"How can you do this without invading Britain, which is unthinkable, especially as many oligarchs are now based there and invested in Britain and Europe?"

"We don't need to invade. We have a fifth column

within. Many academics promote Marxism at the universities to the gullible youth. A Trotskyite, militant leftist group is undermining Labour and based on its growing influence over government in Liverpool, this could be a model for taking control of other major cities. Sheffield is vulnerable and though Thatcher abolished red Ken Livingstone's greater London Council, there is still a significant core of Socialist militants in London boroughs which we could readily stir into action. Then there is the IRA whose violent activities serve as a proxy military for our cause. Many of their militants are neither Catholic nor truly Irish nationalists. These comprise hard line Socialists and psychopathic criminals who just can't stop killing."

"Well, with these resources in place why are you not going ahead without delay?"

"The reason is simple my friend, they need financing and we have no money, now that our agencies and industries are being disbanded and dissolved. This is where you and your well-heeled friends come in."

"But as many of us live in the UK, and our assets and bank deposits are within the legal ambit of the British government, we are very exposed if we were detected providing such finance."

"We understand this and have long had ways of moving clandestine cash around the world through compliant banks and other channels below the West's financial controls radar."

"But the Soviet Union is finished, so why should we take this enormous risk for no guarantee of your success in restoring Russian power?"

"First of all, comrade, we believe we can appeal to your loyalty to the Rodina, but if not, there are other ways of ensuring your support for our cause."

"What do you mean by your implied threat?"

"To be blunt, the bountiful cash flows from your purchase of former Soviet enterprises and the businesses you control and have invested in, are enjoyed at our discretion. Also, it may not have escaped your attention that one of your breed is currently before our courts, and if convicted he may find himself on the way to reflect over years of hardship in a distant gulag. I can assure you that they have not been disbanded. If all else fails, our long arm still reaches into western havens, and the increasing rate of sudden deaths amongst Soviet defectors must give you pause."

"General you make a very plausible and almost irresistible appeal and I will consult my business associates to see what we can do to help you achieve your goals. I will get back to you as soon as possible."

"Thank you for your cooperation comrade. Your proposal should be with us by the end of this week and I suggest you do not attempt to leave Russia in the meanwhile. We know where you and your family live in London, and I understand you have grandparents and other family members still resident here. I look forward to seeing you again soon and to doing business with you."

When the oligarch had left a staff officer leaned around the office door.

"General, the black arses have arrived."

"Keep them waiting Piotr, I need to report on my last meeting. Give them a compass so that they can find

Mecca, and those carpets in the conference room are of Iranian origin and so sufficiently Halal for them to pray on."

11
CATALAN COLLUSION

Gredos Bar

"Pretty quiet for this time of night, what are you drinking, Cava?"

"The Spanish don't come out to play until after 9 pm when most of the village will turn up, including their kids, you'll see."

The football had brought out an early cluster of fans, but the bulk of the clientele were from the English conversation workshop. The locals looked resentfully at this invasion of foreigners, but their animosity was confined to unfriendly stares and lustful leering at the women. At the suggestion of the owner, who was serving behind the bar and welcomed the additional custom, some of the Spanish participants made contact with the TV watchers and the buying of a round of drinks eased the tension.

Miquel had commandeered a small table in a corner away from the main crush which were busy ordering drinks and starting to dance to loud jukebox music. Ken and Kat soon picked up his intent and drew up two more chairs to make a threesome that invited no intrusion by others.

"Hola, Miquel! Meet my friend Kat. She is working with me on this mission. Her security clearance makes it safe to include her in all we say and agree on."

"Pleased to meet you. I am aware of your MI6 connection, Ken, but perhaps you might like to hear how I fit into your picture, is that the right English expression?"

"Spot on Miquel, and we would appreciate hearing about why you became involved in this."

"Because of the delicacy and danger of your mission, I'm here at the command of the highest level in CESID, Spain's secret service, but you must understand, at the outset, that whilst I accepted this assignment, voluntarily, I am a proud Catalan loyalist and therefore more dedicated to Catalonia's interests and hopeful of ultimate secession from Spanish rule."

"That sounds strange, that a would-be secessionist would agree to hep frustrate Irish nationalists with the same hopes for their country."

"On the face of it that would be true, but my motivations are more complicated than that. Not only would our success frustrate IRA plans it would also damage ETA terrorists who claim to fight for Basque freedoms. Whilst I and the Catalan leadership have sympathy with the separatist political aims of the Basques and the Irish, we cannot accept their violent terrorist methods which go beyond attacks on soldiers and policemen to kill and maim innocent people and especially children."

"So how do you think you can help us?"

"First I have to warn you about the danger facing you if you are discovered by the terrorists and their many informers and collaborators here. I have a message from your people in London — here is the coded message sent via our Madrid office:

'*Your Oldham informant has been savagely assaulted and tortured. He was shot through both elbows and nailed to the floor by his knees, a hallmark IRA punishment for informants. They must have heard of his talking about their operations. Although in a bad way, he has survived, and because they did not kill him and based on what he told us, we believe that the integrity of your cover has not been broken, but it is vital that you are alert to the risk you run if exposed. Your Spanish contact will advise you on further steps to strengthen your cover and protect yourselves.*

Imperative that if you suspect you are blown, abort the mission immediately and we will extract you. If safe to do so, cross the border into Gibraltar where you will be as secure as if you had arrived home. Failing that, we will find you and our Spanish friends will shield you as best they can, without seeming to be involved.'"

Ken knew their task was dangerous, but this message made their danger horribly clear, in all its gory detail. Much as he tried to maintain a neutral expression, Kat registered his shock at reading the message and though aware she should not refer to it in public, she was desperate to find out later what was in it.

"You can see now why you will have to go armed from now on, and I have deposited the sort of weapons you were trained to use before you came here, in your room safe. Have them with you at all times from now on and be sure to wear them discreetly, as you were taught in Derbyshire.

Now back to me and what I can do. Like you, I am an unknown and deniable, not being a recognised member of our secret service. Yet, through my Catalan connections I am well aware of what is being done to keep tabs on terrorist groups operating against and inside Spain. If you go along with the cover of our meeting through the workshop and becoming friends, it will follow naturally that I will offer you hospitality in my home city of Barcelona, and in doing so, guide you to the suspected locations of terrorist and foreign Mafia haunts. Also, I will steer you through any 'Spanish difficulties' you might encounter."

"We are reassured by what you have told us and we are appreciative of the risks you are running to help us. Where do we go from here?"

"We finish the workshop in accordance with the programme. You continue to treat me as a participant in public, but under the guise of conversational improvement, we can maintain contact."

"Thank you Miquel, we are glad to have you on our side."

12
WEB OF TERROR

Barcelona

Kat had been hit hard by the torture of the UK informant but, by the time they set off back to Madrid, she had regained her composure and added an even more steely determination to pay back the bastards who maimed him.

"Ken, isn't Atocha station beautiful, all that greenery in the old station and the Ave trains are so sleek, looking like greyhounds straining on the leash to race away?"

"It puts some of our stations to shame, although the planned work on St Pancras will look good when finished. I am not so impressed with their relaxed attitude to security though. We have learned the hard way what mayhem can be created by a bomb in a waste bin."

The silky smooth run over the high plateau and down to Barcelona was all that the AVE's reputation claimed. A drink in the bar did not even spill over the glass's rim, even when the train hit three hundred kilometres an hour. Country that baked in summer sun was coated with a dusting of snow, making the castles and churches defiantly perched for centuries on high crags, daring enemies to do their worst, look brittle in the freezing air.

Barcelona approached and they feared that this tourist Mecca was also a nest of spies and arms dealers, and for them, if they were not extremely alert, it might be the end of the line. Miquel had been true to his word and now they were armed. Both carried Glock pistols, which they had learned to shoot with on their training course. Ken had a vicious knife in a spring-loaded sheath, up his sleeve and Kat had secreted a stiletto in a discreet part of her person. Neither of them wanted to resort to violence, but they felt more secure having the means to defend themselves against attack, and if their lives were threatened, they were able and ready to kill.

Their meeting with Miquel was in the reserved dining room of the renowned, Cal Pep tapas restaurant, which they entered, shouldering their way past lines of impatient diners waiting to get a seat at the Tapas counter and scowling with envy at these favoured foreigners who were allowed access to the culinary, holy of holies out back. The reception by their maitre d and the rich ambience and floor-to-ceiling wine racks of this jewel of a dining area, confirmed that Miquel was a person of influence and with clout in his home city.

Miquel was already there and seated with another younger man who turned out to be a businessman who, having studied in Wales, spoke excellent English and even some Welsh. Miquel explained that such was the demand to get into the restaurant he had been required to ensure the table was booked for a minimum of four diners. The only jarring note was a noisy table of Danish seafarers who must have bought their way in and were already drinking with Viking abandon. At least they would not be overheard against the noisy outbursts of this boorish band of brothers.

The food was excellent and they even had the personal attention of the maitre d when a large succulent octopus tentacle required carving into bite sized pieces. The wine was equally rich and soothing on the palate. Miquel warned that whilst they could speak freely they should be circumspect when any staff approached their table, as one could not be sure that agents and informers weren't at work, even in such a select hostelry.

"Welcome to Barcelona. I am pleased to introduce my brother to you. Unlike me, he is more of a businessman than political player but he is an equally passionate Catalan and opponent of Basque terrorism, which diminishes the legitimacy of our cause.

It will be good for you to have another contact, especially one who is removed from political affairs and passes for what he is, the owner of a successful and growing cosmetic business. Tomorrow he will take you on the usual visitor's tour of the city and I will join you for a light lunch at a food stall in the central Merkat. Also, we have booked you into a budget hostel, The Three Cats, which is newly refurbished, and although basic, it is bright and clean and close to transport links. All of this will confirm that you are tourists on a tight budget, relying on friendship made at the workshop to give you an insider's look at the city. Be sure to keep up this appearance and don't indulge in drinks or meals at too expensive places and use buses and the metro rather than taxis. Also, stay away from those false Irish bars. They are bound to have behind the scenes links with political Irish."

It was late when they left the restaurant, street lights had been turned off and nobody was about. Together, they walked the few hundred metres to where their vehicles were parked and were saying parting words when, with a roaring engine and squealing tyres, a powerful limousine hurtled around a corner and drove straight at them. With lightning reflexes, Miquel pulled his brother with him into a shop doorway, and with a desperate tackle, Ken shunted Kat onto the pavement and fell on top of her, sheltering behind a telephone kiosk. Before the car sped away round the next bend Miquel shot out the back window, yelling curses after them in what sounded like pretty ripe Catalan.

"Are you alright he asked?" and sighed with relief when Ken and Kat got to their feet and re-joined the others.

"That was close Miquel and well done getting that shot off. It might not have hit anyone, but it will surely persuade them not to come back and try again?"

"That was my intention and a hit would have been an extremely lucky shot considering their speed and the darkness.

"Are you OK Kat?"

"Yes, just a torn stocking and a little bruising due to Ken's heavy tackle but much preferable than colliding with a car fender. Does that mean that we are blown?"

Miquel's brother thought not.

"That was more the style of a mafia hit than a terrorist attack. There would have been more shooting if the IRA or ETA was involved. It was most likely an attempt to take out Miquel, because when in office his government mounted a tough campaign against organised crime and drug barons and they have been threatening payback for some time. Had they hit us, you would have just been collateral damage."

Miquel ushered them into his car and quickly drove away.

"Well, thank God for our escape. That's enough excitement for your first night in Barcelona. You are facing enough dangers without getting caught up in our affairs. Let's get you safely to your accommodation."

13
WHAT A NIGHT

The Three Cats

The hostel was quiet — this was not the season for budget travellers and backpackers. The old, clackety lift carried them up to a Spartan, but bright, reception area and the young man on duty assured them he had allocated them their very best double room which even had an en-suite bathroom. They were tired from the day's activities and Kat was still more than a little shaken and emotionally drained by learning of the IRA's callous brutality, and the near escape from being run down.

They shared a queen-sized bed, both wearing night attire unlikely to rouse their dormant libidos, with Ken under the sheet, beneath the duvet, and Kat above the sheet, creating a suitable chastity barrier. Ken slept soundly but lightly and was aware of Kat getting up to use the toilet. He felt her return to the bed, but it wasn't until she put her arms round him that he realised she was under the sheet and spooned into his back.

"Ken, I am afraid and cold, please hold me and comfort me." Then she let go and burst into tears.

Rolling over he cradled her in his arms and spoke soothing words in her ear.

"That's alright lass, what happened to that poor chap has unsettled me too and it's natural you should feel this way. I am scared too but I must say having the gun on me helps me feel that I have a chance to hit them first if they try anything."

"Oh Ken, you must feel I am a real wuss. I am supposed to be a tough agent, and here I am facing the first threat of danger and falling to pieces. I am afraid that if we are attacked I will let you down."

"I don't think anything of the sort, and from what I remember of your shooting and knife fighting in the training sessions, I would much rather have you on my side than having to face you when your dander is up. Yes, that's the key. Try to turn fear into fury and let the primitive she-cat in you loose on them."

"Your words are encouraging Ken, but I am not sure I share your confidence in my reaction when it comes to the crunch."

"Well, I have seen a fighting mad sheila turn on two big guys who were hassling her in a water front bar in Woolloomooloo. When she glassed one of them, making a real bloody mess of his face, the second ran away like a frightened sheep and all the other men in the bar gave her a wide berth for the rest of the night."

She did not respond, but stopped snuffling, relaxed into his embrace and seemed to be falling asleep, when he realised that her closeness had aroused him and she had reached through the open crotch of his pyjamas and was cupping his balls and firmly gripping his rampant cock.

"I want you Ken, pull off this ugly nighty and fuck me. Fuck me! Fuck me!"

Ken reacted instinctively and having pulled her nightie over her head, reached down probing through her rich thatch to stimulate her more, but she knocked him away and grasping him firmly peeled back his foreskin and thrust him deep inside her. She was so wet and pliant she needed no foreplay and before he could start his rhythmic penetration, strong hands grasped his buttocks urging him deeper and higher into her. With gasps and little cries she urged him on.

"Come on Ken. Give it to me, fuck me hard." Spurring him on, she raked her sharp finger nails across his arse galvanising him into violent thrusting, whilst kneading and nipping her pert breasts.

He had no idea how long this frenzy lasted, but before he could reach his shattering climax, she arched her back, shuddered, clamping him inescapably inside her, whilst orgasmic waves broke over her and screamed like a banshee. Ken collapsed on her, shattered by the demanding effort, but before he could assemble any kind of considered response, he blurted out, irreverently:

"Wow is that what you Aussies call a naughty?"

A flying pillow whacked the side of his head, and Kat, still holding him inside, rolled them both off the bed with a thump, sending them both into paroxysms of hysterical laughter.

When the laughter had died away, they lay on the floor for some time, silently clinging to each other, until cold drove them back to the bed and in a tender embrace, under the welcome duvet, they drifted into blissful sleep.

Although Ken had done the Gaudi thing and all the other tourist's delights of Barcelona, they went along with the tour proposal to reinforce their front, but he was glad when they strolled down Las Ramblas to meet up with Miquel in the glorious Boqueria Market. Miquel was excited about something and as soon as they had ordered snacks and ice cold beers, he was quick to impart his news.

"Tomorrow is Sunday, a good day to get out of town into the country and I plan to show you some of my favourite spots on the Catalan coast. Based on some new intelligence I have received, we can combine this with a visit to a fascinating village with elaborate classical Cuban style villas, built by men who returned from making fortunes trading Cuban cigars. Some of these substantial homes are rented out and at least one is leased to foreigners. Strange comings and goings in the middle of the night have been reported from one of them. The leasing was done through a Spanish agency. All the staff is from Madrid and they are the only people from the house who make contact with locals and their supplies come by truck from Barcelona. We have made discreet enquiries of the delivery company and the supplies seem to be of the usual household variety, excepting for unusually large orders of Vodka and Guinness."

14
ON THE MONEY TRAIL

St Petersburg, Former KGB HQ

"Colonel, bring the Arabs in now."

The Libyan delegation, including its ambassador, entered the office and greeted the General.

"Salaam alaikum, General. It is our great pleasure to be in St Petersburg once more and we look forward to continuing our profitable relationship."

"Dobre utra. Welcome your Excellency and colleagues, are you fully aware of why I have invited you here?"

"We have been fully briefed by our government and understand that you wish to transfer a substantial amount of money, with utmost discretion, to pay for goods we are about to deliver to western revolutionary interests."

"That is correct. It is vital that this transfer is undetectable by interfering British and American electronic surveillance, and evades their international money transfer controls."

"We assume you are referring to the Islamic, Hawala system which for centuries has allowed the faithful to send money and settle debts internationally, without detectable records and hidden from monetary system controls."

"That is correct. It has worked before in funding surprise attacks on western interests by our revolutionary friends, and we have immediate need for you to arrange a substantial transfer to your banks to pay for the supply of necessary arms and munitions."

"We confirm General, that we are willing and able to do this as soon as required and we understand that our Colonel has specified the items that you are requested to provide as part collateral for this financial transaction and in return for our on-going support of your initiatives, especially those against US interests."

"Yes, we are conscious of your vulnerability to American air strikes, since that despicable raid in 1986 and we will ensure that your air defences will be bolstered by the supply of the latest radar and SAM anti-aircraft missile systems, which have proved more than a match for marauding US aircraft."

"Excellent. As soon as the weapons delivery arrangements are confirmed the money transfer will be executed."

"Bolshoe spasibo gentlemen, it is always a pleasure to do business with you. Please extend our most respectful greetings to Colonel Gaddafi."

"Colonel, get onto that spineless money mine from London and tell him we have fixed the means of transferring the finances and whilst he is not to know that we will pay off most of the debt with arms, we need he and his friends' patriotic contribution to boost our depleted coffers, soonest. Or else!"

Tel Aviv, Mossad HQ

Urgent: encrypted message to CIA Langley and MI6 London.

'Our Russian sources have reported siting more than usual Libyan Government delegation presence in St Petersburg. Although KGB is officially disbanded, a dissident group is still working to preserve their clandestine power, and the Arabs have been making contact with the Russian group's leadership.

We are aware that Gaddafi is seeking to upgrade his air defences but the make-up of the Libyan party suggests a focus on non-military collaboration.

We are unable to pursue this more directly but suggest you apply some of your resources to what might be a smouldering fire.'

London, MI6 HQ

"Minister, we have received the attached message from Mossad about alleged Libyan and Russian collusion. We do not know what is being plotted, nor who or what the target might be, but we need your approval to commit some resources to investigating this potential threat."

"Thank you C, for bringing this to my attention. Has GCHQ or the Americans picked up any electronic messaging that might enlighten us?"

"No ma'am. That's why we are concerned. Our eaves-dropping is picking up nothing related to this news."

"Go ahead then. I assume you are referring to agents on the ground and I am sure I have no need to stress the need for the utmost caution and secrecy."

"We are fully appraised of that, and as a result we will be employing the most indirect, deniable and expendable resources."

15
HOMAGE TO CATALONIA

Beguiling, Begur

Much as Ken respected Miquel's commitment and capability, especially after last night's brush with disaster, he was not looking forward to a tour of the highlights of the Catalan coast. Sure enough, even in winter, small groups of lobster-red Brits hogged the outside tables at the seaside cafes in Tossa de Mar, but local know-how saved them from over exposure to his cooked compatriots. Tucking into Jamon Iberico de Bellota followed by whole fresh lobster at Sa Rascassa, and the sea-cliff views from the terrace of the Parador de Aiguablava showcased the less obvious charms and delights of the Costa Brava.

But the jewel in the crown was yet to be revealed in Begur: a delightful mix of twisting, narrow streets of Moorish and Spanish architecture at the foot of a crumbling medieval castle. In addition, and its main delight, was the cluster of neo-classical mansions built by Spanish merchants who had made their fortunes in the nineteenth century Cuban cigar trade.

The Aiguaclara hotel, which was to be their base, was set in a colonial style mansion from the1860s and was a perfect setting for their sight-seeing cover.

"Our people have learned nothing from talking with the staff from the suspect mansion, but a local chemist was heard to laugh at the quantity of high spectrum sun blocking lotion and burn creams being consumed by the residents."

"So it is clear Miquel, that they are not Mediterraneans."

"Absolutely not, nor are they Arabs. I have arranged for you both to go on a guided village tour which stops to take in the front of the house. It will give you a chance to be openly inquisitive and maybe get some clues by peering through the gate. A local boy kicked his football over their garden wall and when he climbed in to retrieve it he was badly scared and almost savaged by a vicious pair of Dobermans. He was saved by the intervention of an armed security guard who spoke very poor Spanish. So, there is no possibility of trying to find out more by trespassing."

The tour had been specially requested, as this was the off-season, and started soon after lunch at a time when summer visitors would have been out of the heat and enjoying a restorative siesta. The female guide was the local librarian and suggested that in the nineteenth century a quarter of Begur's inhabitants migrated to escape poverty and most went to Cuba.

Those who made fortunes returned and built lavish mansions known locally as Casas Indianas. In many cases they were fronted by elaborate wrought iron gates, and inside, the high ceilings and walls were decorated with lavish murals. The stop at the house of interest delivered up little fresh information. It was owned by an absentee landlord and the current tenants ensured their privacy by deploying savage guard dogs and armed guards at night. Some local gossip identified them as publicity shy pop or film stars, and darker rumours feared they were people with much to hide, such as British criminals or East European Mafiosi. The librarian confirmed they were unfriendly and had more money than sense.

It was Kat who came up with the most likely plan for finding out more and one that placed her in great danger. One of the guards at the house was known to take off time to drink at a low-down bar where, although he drank sparingly and talked even less, he had made several passes at local loose women and even scored with one for a steep price.

With her blonde hair dyed black and some subtle changes to her make-up and clothes, Kat entered the bar on the evening of his habitual visits and was readily accepted by the local men as a naïve and possibly available Australian back-packer looking for a taste of Iberian rough trade. She was soon to get her wish when the security man arrived and moved right in on her.

"Want a drink and where you come from?" he enquired in faltering but understandable English.

"Australia mate, and where does a hunk like you come from?" she replied.

He told her he was a sailor on shore leave from a Rumanian registered tanker and that he was spending up his considerable bonus before his leave ran out. He was quite good looking, tall and very strongly built. From his touch on her arms and hands his calloused caresses suggested a manual work background and she suspected he would have a very strong grip if one were to fall into his clutches. It didn't take many drinks to warm him up and he couldn't take his eyes off the cleavage she had contrived to expose more than was wise, in a male dominated bar.

He had been schooled not to blabber, so she learned very little about the house and its occupants, and when she had had enough and he suggested she came to see the beautiful house at which he was staying, she complied and left with him, in the faint hope that she might get into the property. The looks the men gave her as she sashayed out of the bar were a mix of disdain and conspiratorial lust.

It soon became clear that he had no intention of admitting her to the house and as they passed the mouth of a dark and noisome alley, he pushed her in, tripped her and threw her to the ground. The shock and impact of her fall rendered her helpless and when he ripped open her dress and fell upon her she was really in trouble. Whilst Ken had accompanied her at first, she had insisted he did not come into the bar, and most likely he had missed her leaving through a side door. She was no stranger to rough sex of the consensual sort, but she cringed at the feel of his horny hands trying to remove her pants. He was randy and rigid, and she feared what was about to happen as he applied his brute force.

She heaved at him to throw him off, but his weight and strength were too much for her. He unzipped his fly and having opened her with fiercely probing hands, he was lining up to enter her with a violent thrust when he screamed, rolled off, and convulsed with ever more violent contortions, crawled along the alley floor.

Jumping to her feet, Kat stepped over him, bent to retrieve the stiletto that was embedded in his groin and stamped on his balls, for good measure, with the steel shank of her high-heeled shoes, before staggering away leaving him to the night and reflections on his misjudgement in tangling with this sheila from hell.

"You did what?" gasped Ken, whilst Miquel and his brother were convulsed with laughter.

'Where did you leave him? I'd better go and silence him."

Miquel applied a gentle but firm restraint on Ken and told him to calm down and not risk upturning a hornet's nest by committing murder in this tourist hot spot.

"Don't worry Ken, he has suffered sufficiently physically, and in lost face that he will not dare tell his mates or his employer what happened, and unless he finds a compliant doctor he might even bleed to death, depending which bits of him Kat managed to skewer."

After a few single malts, Ken did simmer down and that night, although Kat clung to him especially tightly in bed, sex was far from their thoughts and way beyond their capabilities.

They never did learn what the fate of the errant security man was. But throughout the next day there was a hive of activity at the mansion with trucks and vans coming and going until nightfall. On the following day all was silence and there was no sign of dogs or guards at the gates. A passing enquiry at the main real estate office established that the coop had been flown and that the villa was immediately available for occupancy on very favourable, discounted terms.

Adios Espagne

Their work had confirmed that a foreign group in Begur were up to no good, but as a result of Kat's encounter with the security guard it was considered unsafe for Ken and Kat to continue their enquiries in Spain at this time. The Spanish authorities intended to infiltrate the group through the service company, and as true blue tourists, Ken and Kat decided to conclude their visit to the Iberian Peninsula by crossing into Gibraltar to take in the sights of the rock and the antics of the Barbary Apes. They were sorry to part-company with Miquel and hoped that he would catch up with them sometime in London, or even in Australia, one day, when their work was done.

As they watched the sun go down on this last toehold of the British Empire in Europe, they were blissfully unaware of plans being finalised that would send them from the balmy climes of a Mediterranean winter to a frostier reception far to the east.

16
TO THE FINLAND STATION

London, MI6 HQ

"Congratulations Eliot, you handled the Spanish business with just the right balance of discretion and necessary executive action, and your partner proved to be a devilishly fierce combatant. I appreciate your disappointment at being withdrawn just as you were on the trail of a promising lead, but you are too valuable assets to be compromised at this early stage, and now that your intervention has flushed them from cover we can leave it to the Spanish to watch and find out more about their plans whilst they are on Spanish soil. You will be pleased to know that your report and praise of their help, especially from that Catalan chap Miquel, has gone down well with them and has assured their on-going cooperation in discovering the terrorists' arms trail."

"Thank you sir. I must confess to some disappointment at being pulled out just as we had picked up such a promising lead, and of course, I am wondering why you have called me here without Kat, who deserves even more recognition than me for the success of our assignment."

"Quite so Eliot, but you are not here just for appraisal and it's far too premature for basking in the glow of achievement and medals not yet won. I want you to take on an even harder task in a less friendly place and at first you will be working alone."

"What about Kat?"

"The credibility of your going to Finland depends upon your prior experience and contacts there. As your main contact was a woman who has intelligence experience and whose involvement is blessed by the Finnish government, we thought it more natural for you to go alone, and Douglas will have other tasks to perform before teaming up with you in Russia."

"Finland? Russia? Why am I going there?"

"We have been alerted by a friendly foreign intelligence agency to more than usually regular and intense meetings in St Petersburg between Libyan interests and the rump of the former KGB, which is desperate to preserve its power and influence. It looks as though a money transaction is being planned and no doubt it is aimed at funding terrorism in the west. So, having revealed the munitions trail we now want you to go after the money trail."

"But why go in via Finland?"

"Fins travel to St Petersburg as readily as we go from Birmingham to London, especially in the winter when the best ballet and opera is staged, with stars returned from summer tours in the west. Russian visas are easier to get than in London and many tourists choose this entry point for that reason. So, going this way adds to the credibility of the tourist image we have created, and you're going to study Russian at the Smolny Institute language school for foreigners, in St Petersburg, puts the seal on your cover. Knowing and enjoying a reunion with Milla is an additional advantage and keeps the Fins onside."

"Sending Douglas on her own to catch up with you in Russia enables her again to exploit her proven feminine allure, and to trail her cape amongst the sort of young officers and government officials who might spill useful information."

"What do you expect me to do?"

"Use the anonymity of mixing with other foreign students, and as you will be billeted with a Russian family in a typical suburban tower block, it will be easy for you to blend in and be able to infiltrate academic and other influential circles where useful gossip can be picked up. We want you both to find out all you can about the proposed money trail the KGB will be using to fund its proxy armies in the west.

I don't know how much you know about Bolshevik history Eliot, but it may amuse you to know that Lenin arrived by train at the Finland Station in 1917 to overthrow the fledgling governments' attempts to establish democratic order, and that you will be arriving at the same station to undermine the totalitarian system of government that he helped create. It was at the Smolny Institute, where you will be studying, that Lenin lived from 1917–18 and where he declared the Bolsheviks' seizure of power and takeover of government.

Good luck and take especial care. Russia is a much more dangerous and unforgiving place than Spain."

17
FINLANDIA

Helsinki

At Stanstead airport, Ken lost the argument with the pretty, but adamant, Ryan Air luggage check-in-clerk and paid her the first of the inevitable additional charges that, along with the rail fare from Tampere airport into the centre of Helsinki, would cancel the savings claims of the supposedly lowest cost fare.

In any other country, the prospect of over an hour's train journey through a countryside buried under many feet of snow, maintained in its pristine whiteness by a temperature twenty degrees below freezing, would have been the last straw for a tired airline passenger, still miles from his destination. But the train and the cafeteria bar coffee were hot enough to let Ken relax and watch the winter wonderland whiz by at an impressive speed. His admiration for Finnish Railways' winter performance went up stratospherically when the ticket inspector apologised for the train being two minutes late and hoped they might soon make this up!

Ken was kitted out in the sort of clothing and footwear that would make him indistinguishable from the locals and he had already blessed the inclusion of the cleats in his boots that had saved him from a dangerously, icy, fall. His MI6 masters had once more stressed his need to make a low-key entry into Finland, which he was easily able to do until he opened his mouth to mangle a few almost unpronounceable words of conversational Finnish. He was to learn that so widespread was the natives' excellent command of English, that had he, as a foreigner, possessed an equal facility in their language he would certainly have stood out. Also, on this occasion he was travelling alone.

Whilst Kat was still to play the role of his regular girlfriend, it was judged on this occasion that it would be better if they split up and undertook different initial assignments before meeting up at their common destination.

But on arrival he was met by the beautiful Milla, who had guided his party around Helsinki and the Hermitage on an earlier tourist visit to Finland and St Petersburg. She greeted him warmly and they were soon waiting for the tram that would take them to her apartment in an outer suburb. Yet again, he was amazed to see that the stop's electronic arrivals board was predicting the imminent arrival of a tram, and despite the metres deep snow drifts in the side streets, there it came, exactly on time.

Like many Finns, Milla spoke several languages and her career had embraced overseas postings with the UN, the Finnish Foreign Service and a spell in army intelligence. Whilst not directly involved in Ken's assignment, she was cleared to be briefed on what he was trying to do and her government approved of her assisting him. But her initial plans for Ken's arrival were more about fun than work. She had arranged to take over a friend's country cottage, complete with wood fired sauna and when they had cleared her car of a blanket of snow, they packed the essentials and set off for the forest hideaway a hundred or so kilometres outside Helsinki.

The comfortable cabin was in winter mode and Ken's immediate task was to raid the impressive timber stack and light the stove and start the sauna's heater. Finns make a ritual of the sauna and Milla was no exception. In its ante-room she had provided a picnic of smallgoods including reindeer sausage and the essential, special, sauna beer to avoid excess dehydration. Ken had spent sufficient time with Milla at their last meeting to learn all about her background and to meet with her engineer brothers, one a former French Foreign Legionnaire, and their families. But this was the first time he had been in such an intimate situation with her and he savoured the sight of her nubile, naked, body.

She was short and of a Junoesque stature. The kerosene lamps, accentuated the patina of her dark, golden skin, suggestive of her race's tribal origins in the Ural Mountains. Long, jet-black hair cascaded down across her sumptuous breasts and draping herself provocatively along the sauna's upper bench, her open legs confirmed her hair's natural colouring.

"Welcome to Finland Ken. It's good to have you here and I am glad to see that you too, are excited to see me again. I didn't get to know you as well as I would have liked last time, but I hope you will allow me to explore you more completely, this time."

Ken certainly was manifesting his excitement and arousal at being stark naked with this gorgeous feline, but before he could compose a response she stood up, leaned over, reached out and firmly grasped his engorged member. His lustful eagerness to enjoy her was tempered by his shock at her masterfully direct approach and apprehension about the painful prospect of love making on a hard, duck-board shelf. But Milla was way ahead of him. Raising him to sit on a padding of towels she straddled him, and plunged him deep inside her. The erotic power of her riding and thrusting testified to her strength and fitness, and her raw passion gave vent to delighted shrieks as he thrust back, massaging and tugging on her pendulous breasts, like he would a feisty mare's reins.

When fully sated they lay back and slowly inhaling the hot, dry air they mingled sweat from their every pore. Ken's ecstasy knew no bounds, but before he could drift off into a sensuous reverie, Milla seized him by the arm and dragged him outside, protesting wildly at having to roll in a bank of deep, crystalline snow, a fool-proof way of dampening and shrivelling his ardour.

Ken gulped at his ice-cold beer and felt a rush of restorative body heat drive out the icy cold memory of the roll in the snow.

"God, that was good, and especially you, Milla, thank you for having me and welcoming me so completely."

"I enjoyed you too Ken, and fulfilled a wish to find out whether your short but sturdy stature promised a power to fully satisfy. You certainly do, and for an Englishman you are exceptionally passionate and attuned to a woman's needs and wants. I love the delicate caressing of your silky fingers all over and especially probing up my inner thighs.

Mmmmmm! But enough of these delights, for now, tell me more about what you are trying to achieve and how I might help you."

18
TO THE HERMITAGE

Helsinki

Before leaving for St Petersburg, Milla took Ken to lunch at her former soldier brother's house. Unlike Scandinavians, Finns have a far more nuanced attitude to the Russians and are far from being as pacifist. After serving with a UN contingent, her brother joined the French Foreign Legion, but after being disgusted by their actions in a former African protectorate he wanted out, and only escaped with the determined help of Milla, who disguised him as a catholic monk and smuggled him into a Finnish embassy and then back home.

Ken was amazed how raw feelings ran in favour of, or against, the Soviet era, and Russian interference in Finnish affairs. As a result of Finland's civil war, families were still divided down the middle and a book about a platoon fighting with Germans against the Soviets to recapture territory lost after the revolution is close to the bible in public esteem.

"We are no lovers of the Russians," Milla's brothers assured him.

"It took years to meet their post war reparations and held back our freedom and economic prosperity. Now after Glasnost they purport to be pacific and democratic, but we do not trust the old bear to change its habits. Of course Milla, who has worked in Germany with the UN, is more forgiving, and we hope she is right in giving them the benefit of the doubt."

After an excellent dinner, the men took Ken upstairs to a room full of hunting and fishing gear and proudly displayed their selection of hunting rifles and a wicked looking crossbow. The evening ended with several toasts to Winston Churchill's memory and in praise of the Iron Lady.

Before leaving, the 'boys' gave Ken some rudimentary instruction and practice in firing the crossbow. It was certainly silent and potentially lethal. It was late when they departed, but on this festive night there were lots of people weaving their merry ways home, and Ken was curious about the police and cadets standing at intervals along the main road.

"Looks as though they are ready to head off trouble, Milla."

She laughed and assured him they were there to pick up any incapable drunks and take them to the warmth of the police cells to sober up over-night.

"It would be an enormous social disgrace for us to find someone frozen to death in the morning — unlike the St Petersburgers who dig out what they call 'snow drops' during the spring thaw. These poor souls are drunks who were abandoned to their fate after a big night out in winter."

"You Finns and the Russians certainly have a different attitude to alcohol and drinking than we do in England."

It would have been easy to drive to St Petersburg. In pre-revolutionary times, Finns who provided aristocratic Russians with a range of mechanical and personal services, such as plumbing and tailoring, could catch a tram at the Russian border and ride into the heart of the Tsar's capital. But they chose the train to maintain his cover as an open and innocent tourist.

Milla was to accompany him and act as his guide for the initial days after their arrival. His luggage was light and included a folding, light-weight, but potentially deadly crossbow, strictly for hunting purposes of course. This was a parting gift from the brothers and ensured that although Ken could not easily arm himself in Russia, without drawing unwanted attention, the crossbow could do more than just down a deer.

The train sped through the snowy landscape passing fat looking farm houses and neat villages. It was obvious when they crossed into Russia because of the deteriorating dwellings and rundown communities. There was no doubt which people enjoyed the most comfortable life under their starkly different governing systems.

St Petersburg

St Petersburg is not a Russian city and at times it seems not to be a city at all. Moscow grew around the original log cabins of Viking raiders, but St Petersburg was planned by Peter the Great on an impossible boggy marsh, stabilised by foundations which included the bones of Swedish prisoners of war and forced labourers, who died building it under inhuman conditions.

But despite these unfortunate beginnings, it always

struck Ken more as a Hollywood set than a real city. Wherever one stood, wonderful streetscapes and canal vistas held ones gaze, and within their bounds, fairy tale baroque palaces and churches absorbed ones attention. At times she appeared to be a courtesan flicking up her skirts and urging the visitor to "Look at me! Look at me!"

Ken wanted to drink in the atmosphere and reacquaint himself with its main features. Milla had stayed at the hotel and was to meet him later when the Hermitage had opened. Despite the cold he sat and rested on a park bench and must have nodded off suddenly to be awoken by camera flashes and the excited chatter of a group of American tourists who were snapping an authentic bunch of Russian hobos, at the centre of which sat the perplexed Ken. At least this confirmed how well his dress and unkempt grey beard blended in with the down-and-outs who only differed from him in the stink of their ripe body odours.

Declining the proffered bottle of vodka, Ken broke away and headed to the entrance to the Hermitage. Getting in was a struggle as this was the free entry day for locals. The trick to coping with the Hermitage and its impossible crowds is to have a specific area of interest to aim for on each visit. He knew where to find Milla, standing in the Modernists' area in front of Modigliani's alluring *Reclining Nude*.

"Remind you of anyone Ken?"

"How could I possibly forget?"

"Let's take in your favourites and then I will guide you to where you will be living."

The metro was so different to the tube — no need to 'mind the gap' as the train was completely sealed in its tunnel with access only through auto-opening doors in the wall. The short trip to Primorskaya was quick and after jostling and elbowing back the aggressive locals they rode on a steep escalator up to the surface.

Groups of men were gathered around what appeared to be a bottle shop, smoking and passing round bottles of vodka and beer. Standing out in the snow didn't seem to bother them. Public porta-loos complete with their own attendant and savage looking Alsatian dog, stood ready to provide necessary relief when required. These became social centres in the evening and although their smell was appalling it was at least better than the free-for-all in doorways and alleyways that served before this 'pay for a pee' convenience was provided.

"Look at those crumbling, workers' tower blocks and the refurbished ones next to them. They must belong to developers and the winners in this new enterprise society. Reminds me of the derelict, post-war bombed sites which I played on as a child in Manchester."

Frozen puddles of undrained storm water surrounded them and cracked and pot-holed pavements threatened their ankles.

"Watch out Ken for those steel rods sticking out from the cracked pavers. They could cause a nasty fall and you don't want to have to visit a Russian hospital."

Amongst all this, stall holders were selling everything from kitchenware, green groceries and fruit, to gigantic floral bras.

"Gee Milla, even you would get lost in those. The estate

must be full of former Soviet Olympic lady shot putters and hammer throwers, or is it their drunken men they toss around?"

"Don't joke about that Ken, domestic violence here is even worse than where we come from."

In the badly neglected scraps of park, surrounding the blocks, packs of mangy cross-bred dogs hung about foraging in the snow covered ground, looking for diversion and perhaps non-Russian speaking prey.

"Look. There it is. That's where you will be living."

"Looks more like a fortress than a home."

The first sight of his new Russian home was an iron gateway which gave access to the fortified block. They had to negotiate three steel doors, including the outer one and an extremely foul smelling lift to gain the comparative security and homeliness of his hostess' apartment on the sixth floor.

Svetlana was a retired chemist who let a room in the flat she shared with her crippled son, to augment their income and pay the bribes necessary to get him timely hospital treatment.

At least he had a room to himself, whilst his landlady shared a room with her grown-up son, and spent most days in her kitchen, with windows that never seemed to open, following the soaps on TV and reading her bible. Shower water was plentiful and hot, but he always had to remember not to clean his teeth in tap water containing giardia and heavy metals. What with this, smoking and alcoholism, it was no wonder average male life expectancy was less than sixty.

The only other house rule he was urged to comply with

was not to whistle, as she feared this could destroy her wealth.

As he farewelled Milla, Ken mused, "I am certainly embedded in the local community here. Let's hope it's as safe as it feels warm and friendly."

"Take care Ken. We Finns have long experience of how Russian hospitality can turn so easily to aggression and occupation — especially when the vodka runs out."

19
A CUNNING COLLEEN

St Petersburg — An Irish Pub

"Sure my ancestors came from Ireland, not with the first fleet mind you but there are stories of their being in dubious businesses including the jumping of the odd gold field claim. But another branch stayed on the straight and narrow, and would you believe it were peelers and magistrates."

"Now isn't that a typical Irish story and what brings you to St Petersburg in the winter?"

"I wanted to experience it in the snow, it's less crowded and I am joining my boyfriend on a Russian speaking course at the university. How about you? You're a long way from the Erin isle."

"Strictly business in my case, you see I have shares in the ownership of this Irish pub you are standing in."

"That must be a leap of faith. I know that the Irish left in huge numbers for America, but I am unaware of there being a Russian connection."

"It's younger than the American link and goes back to the revolutionary days which coincided with our uprising against English suppression. The Bolshevik government supported us by sending money and arms and some say that link is still strong with the IRA, some of whom are more inclined to Communism than Catholicism."

"So does your pub and drinkers contribute to the cause?"

"Lord no. Even to this day, Special Branch watch Irish abroad like hawks, and now that the USSR has collapsed, the new government is anxious not to pick a fight with the west, especially now and since the recent Manchester bombing. The nearest we get to the troubles is the singing of rebel songs at our Friday night folk bashes. You should come along, alone preferably, but bring your boyfriend too if you must."

"Thanks, I think I will. My name's Kat, what's yours?"

"Fergus. Grand to meet you and I will look forward to buying you a dram on Friday night. You might even meet some relatives."

Kat could barely hear herself think for the blast of noise that hit her as she entered the pub. The seething mob of well-oiled drinkers was mostly responsible, but as an undertone to their boozy bellowing, an amplified Irish folk group belted out patriotic nationalist numbers without any of the inhibition that a performance in an English pub might necessitate.

A firm but friendly grip on her arm turned her towards the smiling Fergus who led her through the throng and into a quieter and obviously private dining room at the back of the pub.

"Sorry about that row. It's worse than usual as Ireland is playing England in Dublin tomorrow, and even in St Petersburg we have die-hard rugby fans who like to get in the right mood even a day before the game. Thought you might appreciate something to eat too, the fare is better in here and you might like to meet some of our Russian friends."

"Thanks. Very kind of you. I could not have stood that torrent of noise for long and it would be good to get the Russian perspective on Anglo-Irish relations."

"Here meet Dimitri. He won't admit it, but he used to work for the KGB."

"Dobry vecher miss. Don't believe this Irish trouble-maker, he has been drinking potcheen with his rebel friends out back before you came in. He likes you and was getting up courage. We Russians know how to treat a lady properly and don't need what you call Dutch courage to greet one properly."

With which, as he was already standing, Dimitri took her hand, bent from the waist and grazed it ever so slightly with a kiss.

"Well I never. Blarney and Russian aristocratic charm in an Irish pub. Not at all like an Australian hotel. There are still some bars there that discourage women from going in, but strangely the bar staff are all female. Good evening to you Dimitri and now that Fergus has given me a glass, here's cheers."

"Na zdrowie! Welcome to Russia. I hope you like it despite the cold."

"I like it very much and will like it even more if there are no jokes about kangaroos in Australia's main streets and you don't call me a sheila."

"Sheila? What is this please?"

"You don't want to know Dimitri. It's an impolite name for an Australian woman. I must go and see that all is well with the band and that the drinkers are behaving themselves. Please enjoy steaks on the house — don't touch the Irish stew, the chef is a Chechen."

"So what do you really do for a living Dimitri?"

"I am in the security business. Now that we have so many millionaire oligarchs living the good life and showing off their wealth, they need protection from our mafia, that's if they are not part of the mafia themselves, in which case we protect them against rival gangs. You will understand that with the end of the Soviet Union many of the former state security officers found themselves out of work and who better to offer security to the new aristocracy."

"So you were with the KGB?"

"Not exactly, more a type of military intelligence but nonetheless aware of the underworld in St Petersburg, and certainly well trained in coping with criminal violence."

Dimitri's English was excellent and as he had been posted in Berlin, he spoke fluent German as well. He was polite, smartly dressed, which suggested a better than average Russian income and certainly was a big step up from the thug she had put down in Begur.

As Fergus had not returned when they had finished their meal, Dimitri asked whether she would like to hear some authentic Russian music in a club that was close to her hotel. As this was in a reasonably up market part of the city, and really close to her hotel, she accepted his invitation and was even more reassured when she stepped out of the pub and into a chauffeur driven late model Mercedes.

The night cub was first class with authentic Russian folk music and dancing, interspersed with opportunities for patrons to try their more conventional and sedate skills on the dance floor. Dimitri and Kat were both competent dancers and whilst he stuck to gentlemanly priorities, she did allow him the occasional squeeze and brush of cheek on cheek.

Getting him to talk was easier than she had expected and at least two bottles of Georgian champagne were a most effective conversational lubricant.

"I am surprised that with the change of government you say that there are some KGB factions still in existence."

"Yes. Old habits die hard and these men who had enormous power and exceptionally comfortable life styles are loath to give them up. We have reason to be wary of them and sometimes have either to pay them off or undertake unsavoury assignments for them which they can deny responsibility for."

"Goodness, surely you don't mean contract killing and that sort of thing?"

"No, we are careful not to go that far, especially as they could hold that over us, to blackmail us into slipping deeper into the mire, where even they can no longer tread with impunity. For instance, we might rough up or scare off foreign interests who are not keeping to a bargain and especially when they want to control or punish Russians living abroad."

"Sounds full of political danger to me and you must find you are serving two masters at times."

"This is especially the case with the oligarchs who live fat cat lives in London. The KGB die-hards tap them for funds and threaten dire consequences for those who don't cough up. There is something going on at the moment. One of our big clients is being pressed to come up with some serious money, which will be intended to finance some illegal activity, and at the same time we are being retained to scare them into complying."

"I don't understand what can the KGB men want with such large amounts of money and why would the overseas oligarchs pay up?"

"How do you think terror groups like the IRA, ETA in Spain and the Red Army brigades in Germany and Italy get money to acquire weapons and explosives? The oligarchs pay up because we are used to get to them and threaten their families who still live here."

"Is that how the IRA will have financed their Manchester bomb?"

"Most certainly and I think they are planning something equally big soon because the oligarchs have been called on and ordered to provide a very big sum."

Kate couldn't believe her luck and was careful to move the conversation to less contentious subjects until it was time to go.

She was happy to accept his offer of a lift to her hotel and was relieved that he had not suggested a night cap at his place. There was also the reassuring presence of his chauffeur. Even so they stopped short of the hotel in a quiet street where the chauffeur got out to buy cigarettes. When Dimitri started to snuggle up to her she allowed him to kiss her and put his hand inside her bra to fondle her hardening nipple, but when she felt a hand lift her skirt and start to track its way between her legs and up the inside of her thigh, she drew the line and he accepted her resistance with a genial laugh and withdrew his hand.

"I have really enjoyed this time with you Kat and I hope we can do this again soon and get to know each other even better."

"I enjoyed it too Dimitri and that would be nice. I look forward to it."

By this time the chauffeur had returned and at a signal from Dimitri completed the drive to the hotel's front door. Dimitri jumped up and rushed around to open her door and Kat stepped out, squeezed his arm meaningfully, pecked him on the cheek and wished him, "Good night Dimitri."

20
SOMETHING'S NOT RIGHT

Belfast bar

"I think we might have a problem, boss."

"What problem would that be, Seamus?"

"We have had to pull out of that safe house we leased in Begur, near to the Catalan coast. The service staff we hired reported that other outsiders had been asking questions about us and they even approached our people. They gave nothing away and all seemed quiet when one of our security men was set upon in the village and he was so badly hurt he bled to death before we could get him to hospital."

"Did he say who attacked him?"

"No. When we found him he was barely conscious and was reluctant to say anything for some reason. He was in terrible pain, one of his balls was crushed and he was bleeding heavily from a deep puncture in his groin. We pressed him hard but before we could get any sense out of him he became delirious and died of blood loss."

"I assume you made enquiries about his movements in the village."

"We traced him to a bar. The locals at first were un-willing to help us but a few rounds of drinks loosened their tongues and it seems he had picked up an Australian woman who appeared to be trawling for some rough trade. He left with her and that's the last anyone heard of him or the woman, she disappeared at the same time. The local Police got wind of it and we told them as little as possible, but it would not have been long before the Guardia Civil took an interest so we packed up and got out the next night, leaving no forwarding address."

"The inquisitive people and the attack on your man might have been a coincidence, but too much is at stake to have risked staying on. You were right to have got out so quickly. But it is a damned nuisance, as that was an ideal base from which to prepare to bring the arms in from Morocco. You had better stay out of Spain and lie low for a while. I will get in touch with our Russian friends — they will be able to find out whether we are under security surveillance."

St Petersburg — former KGB HQ

"General, we have heard from the IRA that they have had to pull their people out of the Spanish safe house and they have asked whether they are under surveillance by some security agency."

"What made them pull out?"

"Questions were being asked about them by people from outside the village and one of their security guards was attacked and killed."

"Are they sure it wasn't some local vendetta for something the guard had done. Perhaps he had molested a local woman, you know how hot-headed those Spanish peasants can be."

"They thought that at first but it seems that an Australian woman was seen with him before he was attacked and she vanished without trace."

"In that case we should take no chances. Send messages out to our contacts and former overseas allies enquiring about this mysterious Australian woman."

"At your command, General."

Cheltenham, GCHQ

"We have picked up a number of signals between Russian interests enquiring about an Australian spy who has been operating against their interests in Spain."

"Doesn't mean anything to me, but we had better forward it to MI6 in case they have such a person in the field."

"Yes sir. I will get on to it straight away."

London, MI6 HQ

"This is a worrying development so early in this operation, and whilst they don't seem to have found out who she is yet we had better warn Eliot and Douglas to be extra careful, especially now they are inside the KGB's front yard."

"I will do that C, but they are still vague about her description and hopefully they will soon make a sufficiently vital breakthrough to justify pulling them out of danger."

Belgrade, Serb Intelligence HQ

"I see that our former KGB colleagues have nothing better to do than pursue an Australian groupie trawling for rough sex in a Spanish bar."

"Still the same old KGB paranoia. If they had focused on what really mattered in recent years both of our federations would still be in business. What can a single Australian girl do to upset our plans?"

"I don't know Novak, but I do remember what one nosey man did to completely destroy our campaign against the Croat lunatics in Australia a few years ago. We certainly underestimated him, to our cost. He caused the death of one of my best friends and a Russian woman agent. I would certainly like to catch up with him again one day."

21
AT THE SMOLNY

St Petersburg

The ride in a rusty, dilapidated mini-bus, crewed by a couple of swarthy Chechens, reminded him of travel in similar primitive mode going through Indonesia on his way to Oz. But in this free enterprise supplement to the city bus service, he was surprised to see how well-dressed the passengers were, obviously professionals on their way to work. It was hard to tell what the fare was, but people passed money forward from the rear seats to the driver who continued to drive whilst scrabbling for change, which was then passed back to the payer.

His first sight of the Smolny Institute reminded him of the worst Baroque excesses of Imperial Vienna. A veritable wedding cake, coated with blue and white 'icing'. What went on inside was far from sweet and enticing.

Ken had hoped he could get by with his most basic Russian phrases and hopefully build on them sufficiently to order food, read metro and street signs, and exchange basic greetings with the locals. This was not to be.

He was soon disabused of that idea by a grim lady tutor who, when not fielding calls from her alcoholic, artist husband, insisted he would learn grammatical Russian or not at all. She even gave him homework. Horrid memories of desperate homework finishing in the bike sheds at North Manchester Grammar School made him shudder at the prospect of returning to this most didactic of learning approaches. Even so, his dunce-like descent from class to lower class marked him out as what he claimed to be — a mature dabbler in foreign cultures and their languages.

Kat was to meet with him at a beer kiosk on the upper gallery of Gostiny Dvor, a department store complex built in the eighteenth century on the foundation of an ancient souk, where camel trains from the east came to off-load and trade their Asian goods. On a summer's day, getting there would have been a charming walk along the Nevsky Prospekt but, with its covering of snow, it appealed much less than the bus ride. It mattered little as the outdoor café tables were snow bound and there was no sign of the high-stepping, gorgeous, fillies babbling away on high end cell phones and flashing their designer brand shopping bags to proclaim where they could afford to shop.

"Hi Ken, it's so good to see you again, I have missed you."

"Me too Kat. I'm glad you have got here safely."

The words and embrace were warm and genuine but both were conscious of their dalliances with others that had occurred since their last being together and they felt a degree of reserve towards each other. Necessity and professionalism took over and Kat brought Ken up to date with her achievement in hooking a Russian on the inside of the mafia-KGB alliance.

"I don't know whether to praise you for your bravery and cunning or lament your death wish in trailing your coat amongst those devils. But do be careful we don't want a repeat of the Bogur incident. It will not be as easy to get away from here in one piece."

"Ken, you wouldn't be trying to diminish my achievement by any chance?"

"Certainly not. I am full of admiration, but also fearful for your safety when you go it alone like this."

"I am a big girl. So what do we do now?"

"Clearly we need to follow the thread you have snagged to lead us closer to the terror source, but it's dangerous and I need to be in a position to act as the cavalry should it all go wrong. In the meanwhile, we had better let London know what you have found out and what we propose doing."

London, MI6 HQ

"That's great news C. So the new kids have pulled it off."

"Yes. Getting inside the enemy's lines on their own territory is a great coup, but to get the extra information will be highly dangerous, especially for Douglas who will be very exposed."

"I am taking immediate steps to put together an extraction plan, and that will have to involve our assets in Finland and the Baltic States, as using Russian-based people will risk alerting the opposition."

22
CARE TO DANCE?

St Petersburg, the Mariinsky Theatre

Dimitri could not have chosen a better venue to win Kat's affection and melt her resistance. The touring stars of the ballet were back and the house was packed with most discerning dance lovers, both locals and many from Finland and even further afield. He was his usual charming and gentlemanly self until, during the closing minutes of the performance, when they were hidden from view in the darkened box, she felt his fingers teasing her inner thigh. This time she did not resist and his further foreplay released her flood and suggested he might win his prey.

He lived in a well-heated old apartment with high ceilings and ornately papered walls of the Tsarist era. He took her coat and when he returned in his shirt sleeves, she was standing behind a large chesterfield couch, leaning forward to better take in a large oil painting of Volga boatmen on the opposite wall. He came up behind her, enclosed her in his arms and began to kiss and nip the skin at the nape of her neck. He was so skilful and quick that the lifting of her gown and dropping of her panties were irresistible, even had she wanted to deny him. Following this, he entered her massively from behind. At first she shuddered with shock at the deep penetration, but as he thrust back and forward with increasingly powerful and deeper thrusts, she gasped and cried out passionately, at the same time pleasuring herself, urging him to give it to her "harder and more! More!"

It was close to dawn when she awoke in his bed, where their frenzied love making seemed to have gone on all night. He was no beardless youth, but his powers of recovery had amazed and delighted her, and it had required all that she could to contain and satisfy his lust for her. His 'little deaths' had drained all his energy, and so dulled his professional caution that her guileful questioning had encouraged him to tell her all about the recipients of the money, what they were likely to do with it, and how they would acquire the munitions and arms necessary to carry out the attack.

The drops she had squeezed into his last glass of champagne had knocked him out completely and he would not wake for many hours. Sending the coded message to Ken announcing completion of the job and her urgent need to be picked up, she dressed and descended to the outer door and slipped out cautiously onto the still darkened street.

She savoured a feeling of smug satisfaction at the memory of his pulsating warmth, still radiating inside her, when a silk scarf encircled her neck and began to throttle the life out of her. But the would be assassin had caught her protective wrist in his garrotte, and it was thanks to the silver bangle she was wearing, a farewell gift from her father, that she was able to still breathe and delay the inevitable strangulation. He had placed his knee into her back to get sufficient leverage that might break her neck, when a thrumming sound, followed by a solid thud, ended her agony and she blacked out. The black clad archer tore the crossbow quarrel from the back of the assailant and cut his throat to ensure he could tell no tales. Milla wiped the blood from her blade on the would-be killer's coat. Ken emerged from the shadows, picked up Kat and carried her away.

Private medical evacuation ambulances were not uncommon visitors to the border crossing with Finland, carrying overindulgent western men and women who had narrowly survived fatal heart attacks, and were being ferried across to receive superior treatment in a western hospital. The one carrying Kat was readily accepted as part of this occasional traffic, and as her impeccably forged papers confirmed her Swedish citizenship, she was waived through by the cold and sleepy border guards.

London, MI6 HQ

"Douglas has done it and thank God, she has come out of Russia alive, though badly scathed and she has got the information about the transmission of the munitions from North Africa to Eire."

"Good girl! Great news C, and I must say, it's a relief that our faith in the unlikely couple has been more than justified. We must move quickly to get them back here and ensure they are untraceable by the opposition who must be hearing disquieting news from St Petersburg."

"As soon as she is recovered enough to travel we have a safe house ready for their de-briefing. They will need to be kept out of circulation for the remainder of this exercise to prevent the Russians or Irish from joining the dots. Despite having searched their networks for information, they have not yet confirmed that the various reports of an Australian woman are about our one and only Kat."

"Good show DG. We have reacted strongly to the Russian decoy operation in Poland, and they appear convinced that we have been duped by one of their much vaunted maskarovkas, and our strategy of not using our known people in Spain and Morocco has lulled them into the false belief that we are not alert to their little game. I suggest we set up a control team to coordinate our watch over the terrorists' movements and any intervention we decide upon. It might be a good idea to incorporate Eliot and Douglas on a needs-to-know basis, as they have been involved from the start and it will keep them out of mischief and harms way. Now, I had better get my skates on to inform the Minister, before her minions get wind of it and start to claim some of the credit."

Helsinki, Military Hospital

"How are you feeling Kat?"

"Oh Ken. It's so good to see you. I am feeling less sore. Come here and give me a hug but gently, I am still a little fragile."

"You will want to cover your throat for a while, but the worst of the bruising and discolouration has gone. You will soon be looking and functioning as new."

"Why am I suspicious of your flattery? What dire news are you shaping up to tell me?"

"Not guilty. The good news is that we are to be whisked

away to a safe house out of London, and that we will be drafted into the coordinating team that will watch over the munitions transfer to its destination. So, we are still in the game, but not in the front line, though it is hoped that we have not been identified as possible agents."

"That's great. I hoped we would not be shut out, but I must confess I will not be ready for more close encounters with the enemy for some time."

"Rest assured, our high and mighty masters are delighted with our work and you are very much the heroine of the hour. But I am afraid Kat there is some unfortunate news that I know will hurt you. Dimitri's body was found floating in the Moyka Canal. It seems that his Mafia bosses, who set the assassin on you, punished him for his indiscretion and used his death to send a message to others in their ranks and to assure the KGB and IRA that they had not lost control of their people. I'm very sorry. I know that whilst he was working for the other side you had formed an attachment and would not have wanted this."

Kat did not cry, but all traces of joy left her face and she sat silently, taking in what he had said. After a while she thanked Ken for breaking it to her gently, before she heard it from less sensitive sources.

"Thanks Ken. I have to be professionally detached about my seduction of Dimitri, but he was a very warm and considerate lover and I can't help feeling some responsibility for his death."

"I understand Kat. It's a reasonable human reaction. At the same time, be assured that you made the breakthrough that will save countless innocent lives."

St Petersburg, former KGB HQ

"I regret that one of our people, indeed one of your former officers, has been indulging himself with an unknown foreign woman. He appears not to have done anything that would betray your operations but as an assurance that we do not take chances when working for you he has suffered the extreme consequences of his foolishness."

"I am glad you have let me know. You will appreciate we were curious about the militia report of the body in the Moyka and even more so about the dead assassin you are reported to have disposed of after his failure to kill the mystery woman."

"Comrade General, your trust in us is vital to our collaboration, and I had hoped to meet with you before you heard about these deaths from others. But you will appreciate my coming to you now is confirmation that we have nothing to hide from you. We intended to close off any possibility of Dimitri having leaked information by terminating the woman as well. But it seems she had protection and they intervened to save her. A classy whore would have that kind of back up. Naturally, we checked on where she went, and as she was wounded by our man, she must have gone into Finland for medical treatment. We have been unable to pick up her trail there. We have assumed that if she were a foreign agent and had passed on information, her handlers would have reacted by now and you would be aware of this."

"I think you have been very fortunate that information appears not to have leaked. To divert attention from our true intentions we launched a very credible maskirovka which suggested that we were about to mount an operation to destabilise Poland, and judging by the increased presence of British and American agents there, and Polish military alerts, they have swallowed the bait. There has been no sign of their showing interest in our dealings with our IRA friends and they have not committed assets on the ground in North Africa or Spain. We are still making enquiries about the woman, both in Australia and in Europe, but she has not been identified as a known agent. So, on this occasion, Alexey, you are forgiven, but you must know that any repeat of this laxness in your work will have the most serious consequences for your organisation and for yourself."

"Your forbearance is much appreciated General. Your message is loud and clear and all of our people are well aware that Dimitri's fate awaits those who transgress. That cocky Irishman who fixed Dimitri with the woman has been warned, and this will ensure his IRA masters don't overreach themselves by straying onto our territory."

Belfast bar

"Seamus, what the hell is going on in St Petersburg? Fergus was set upon by some street thugs and they say he will not walk again?"

"We don't know boss. Word is that he could be a bit fly and that he may have trodden on mafia toes, either through his liquor supply activities undermining their interests, or even worse, his rival drug dealing."

"The KGB boyos don't seem too concerned, and the good news is that the money has been transferred and the munitions supplies are good to go."

23
GAME ON

Cheltenham, GCHQ

"With all the targets we could monitor, why do we waste our time tracking government bank deposits?"

"It's a trip wire system. World Bank regulations require any country seeking to qualify for international loans to prove that their Central Bank is solvent. They have to record significant cash flows and any unusual movements or deposits, which can give us advance warning of the funding of dodgy activities."

"Like this unusually large sudden accumulation of funds from a variety of unidentified sources in the Libyan Government account?"

"Absolutely old son, and as that is one account we have been specially warned to keep an eye on, we had better get word of it to Financial Services straight away.

London, MI6 HQ

"The money's in the bank Kat, and the coordinating team has the go ahead to take action."

"It will seem strange to be in the background, but at least we will be able to follow the game and see the ultimate outcome of our work."

Kat and Ken entered the control room, where the London based coordinators sat before a cluster of screens showing real-time developments in Spain and North Africa. To their delight, Miquel was just completing his report from Barcelona and had time for a few words.

"Hola my friends. Congratulations on your Russian work. Thanks to you we have a clear lead on where the munitions trail starts and when the cargo will be approaching Spanish territory."

"Hi Miquel. Good to see you in action again. But aren't you afraid that your observers will be spotted and give the game away?"

"No. We are not concerned. Our way of watching them involves local assets who are part of the natural social landscape, and even if detected their discovery would not lead to us. I must go now to keep up with our people, but you can follow the action on your screens. Good wishes and I hope we can catch up again when all this is over."

"Thank you Miquel. Ken and I look forward to sharing more of your city's excellent hospitality. Go well and safely. Best wishes to your brother."

North African coast

The convoy of trucks negotiated the border crossing from Algeria into Morocco without incident. The Libyan authorities had taken suitable steps to lubricate their passing. The road was busy with commercial trucks, and where the irrigated farms gave way to arid uplands, wandering Berber shepherds and goatherds tended their flocks. On a rocky outcrop, commanding an extensive view of the highway, a group of tribesmen had stopped under tree shade to rest and enjoy a mid-day meal. They were so much part of the roadside scenery that the truck drivers barely noted their presence.

A closer look would have revealed two of the party, sitting away from the rest, who were intent on signalling via a satellite phone to their base in Ceuta. Although indistinguishable from the other tribesmen, these were a special breed of men, attuned to the nomad life, but belonging to the Spanish Foreign Legion, the feared 'bridegrooms of death', and loyal to Spain. They were communication specialist officers of the BOEL special operations forces which had been charged with keeping tabs on the convoy as it crossed Morocco and into the Spanish enclave of Ceuta.

Ceuta

News of the convoy's arrival in Ceuta had been signalled to Madrid, and as the cargo was designated — arms for the Spanish military — the trucks were secured in the Legion barracks. After days on the road and camping by their vehicles, the drivers welcomed an invitation to enjoy the comforts of canteen food and barrack room beds. This enabled Legionaries suitably camouflaged for night operations, to move from truck to truck, checking the contents of each crate and marking them electronically to ensure they could be traced should any part of the cargo be diverted in Spain, rather than delivered on to Ireland.

St Petersburg, KGB HQ

"What news of the convoy, Piotr?"

"All has gone smoothly, General, the Libyans fixed

the border crossings and there has been no sign of any watchers. The crates are to be loaded tonight and shipped on to southern Spain. They will then be trucked north and the consignment for ETA will be dropped off. The rest will be loaded onto a Chinese freighter that makes regular sailings between Santander and Cork in Southern Ireland."

"Some good news and efficiency at last. What arrangements have been made to ensure there are no problems with Irish authorities?"

"Once the ship leaves the Spanish port the safe arrival of our cargo is the responsibility of the IRA. They assure us that they have arranged for there to be no trouble with the Irish coast guard and customs authorities, and one of their men is travelling with the cargo to ensure there are no slip-ups."

"Excellent. I think that calls for a drink, Piotr. Keep me informed of the consignment's safe arrival in Ireland."

24
SEA TRAIL

London, Foreign Office

"The cargo is heading for Spain, Minister. Part of the consignment will be off-loaded in Spain for ETA, and the main part will then be trucked to a Spanish port and shipped across to Ireland."

"Well done C. So far this operation has gone better than I thought possible, but now comes the very delicate part. It is vital that the Spanish do not jump the gun in dealing with their terrorists, and we must keep tabs on those arms and explosives, without the Irish Government knowing of our involvement."

"I have the strongest assurance from the Spanish that they will not move until we advise them our operation is concluded, with the proviso that should ETA be about to mount an attack, they will feel free to act. We have alerted the Special Boat Service to monitor the shipping between Spain and Ireland, and once it has landed there the SAS will take over surveillance in such a way that their involvement is most clandestine and readily deniable, should they come under suspicion. To a large extent high-flying drones and satellite surveillance are likely to be employed rather than risking people on the ground."

"That sounds good, but you must be careful to avoid causing a diplomatic embarrassment and when I remind you that the Queen will be attending the Trooping of the Colour ceremony, you will appreciate how vitally important it is that the cargo does not disappear from our view."

"Yes ma'am. We feared she might be a target, and you can be assured we have all contingencies covered."

Poole Dorset, SBS HQ

"As discussed Commander, we now have the green light to plan close, but undetectable, surveillance of the cargo about to be ferried from Santander to Cork. The lead time is necessarily short and you are advised to co-opt SAS, RAF and GCHQ assets in case their involvement is required. I don't need to tell you how critical and secret this operation is."

"Yes Admiral. We have been working on some options with our colleagues in the other services and I intend letting you have our proposal within twenty-four hours."

"Good. But make sure there is no slippage in your planning as the consequence of missing the possible attack deadlines is unthinkable."

Cork, IRA Safe House

"All goes well with the consignment, boss. We dropped off the ETA supplies without incident. I am about to board the Chinese freighter and we should soon be safely docked in Cork."

"Good man Sean. Keep a close eye on the crew and make sure none of them gain access to the sealed hold where our goods are. We look forward to greeting you."

Somewhere in the Atlantic

"Why is that patrol boat signalling us to slow down? You told me there would be no problem getting into Ireland?"

"Don't panic Captain. That is a friendly Irish coast guard boat. It is normal for them to check up on vessels, and we have arranged for their making a short and favourable inspection of your boat. There will be no trouble and any illegals amongst your crew need not worry. They will want access to the locked cargo hold for forms sake — they know what it contains and will raise no objections. Now, get ready to assist them in coming alongside and boarding us."

The three officers who came aboard were full of welcoming bonhomie, and as Sean had predicted, their inspection was brief and businesslike. Two of the men, wearing coveralls and carrying canvas bags, went below to make the cargo inspection, while their spokesman remained on the bridge chatting with the captain and Sean.

"Thank you, Captain. All appears to be in order. You are about to enter Irish waters, so it is appropriate to welcome you and your crew to Ireland, and as I have a flask of Bushmills single malt with me, perhaps we might share a dram to celebrate your safe arrival."

When the patrol boat cast off, the freighter resumed its course for Cork.

"Well, as promised Captain, that was painless and those boys were very easy going — not at all starchy as those Royal navy bastards are. Funny though, could have sworn one of the inspection guys had a trace of Belfast accent.

But I guess many of the republican persuasion have come to live in the south and I have certainly met some in the Garda. Now for Cork where you will find the customs officials equally accommodating. They understand that the cargo is destined for the Irish military."

Poole Dorset, SBS HQ

"All went smoothly at sea, Admiral. The ship landed the cargo in Cork and what appeared to be Irish military trucks left the dock, carrying the consignment. We have fulfilled our orders sir, and now it's over to the RAF and foot sloggers to keep tabs on them."

"Thank you commander and well done. Congratulate your men on my behalf."

Cork, IRA Safe House

"Well done Sean. The cargo has been split up and will be stored partly in a warehouse on a Cork industrial estate. The rest is destined for an unoccupied former monastery in a remote valley of the Wicklow Hills. We are ready now for the call to action that will really shake the British out of their complacency. Our Russian friends will think their money well spent."

London, MI6 HQ

The mood in the coordinating group control room was buoyant.

"The navy boys have shepherded the cargo into the hands of the IRA and now we know where it is cached."

"They did a good job Ken, in keeping tabs on it and without being detected by the Russians or the IRA. I have no idea what comes next, but MI6 seem very pleased with their selves and so I assume there is more to come. But we are unlikely to be involved."

25
TRAIL'S END

London, Hampstead Café

Ken and Kat enjoyed lazy Sunday mornings. She was reading the weekend papers from cover to cover, whilst he over-indulged in a 'full Monty' fried breakfast, including all the trimmings, but without chips. On the TV over the bar, the *Andrew Marr Show* droned on about the week's political happenings when, suddenly, an announcer cut in to deliver urgent breaking news.

'News is coming in of two massive explosions in the Republic of Ireland. A warehouse on a Cork industrial estate, and a disused monastery in the Wicklow Hills near Dublin, have been totally destroyed by explosions which occurred, almost simultaneously, a short time ago. Garda and fire service units are on the scene, but they have not yet released any information about the blasts, other than to confirm that there has been no loss of life or injuries to people. The Taoiseach is scheduled to front a televised news conference at around noon today when more will be known about these violent incidents.'

"My God! There was a plan B. But how did they do it and go undetected?"

"I don't know Kat. But the Russians and IRA will

be fighting mad and looking for culprits and revenge. We had better get back to the safe house and hope to be summoned by our bosses to a briefing. Let's go."

Poole, Dorset, SBS HQ

The Dorset base wardroom was packed with joint services brass and the SBS, SAS and RAF men and women involved in the recent operation. The bar was struggling to meet the demands for drinks when all were urged to charge their drinks by the Admiral responsible for the naval service.

"I stand here today bursting with pride at what you have achieved to protect our people from the scourge of terrorism without loss of life. What you have done is particularly admirable, in these times of budget cuts, supply constraints, and general retrenchment of military resources. Despite this, it is taken for granted by our political masters and a grateful public that Special Forces will always rise to the challenge. You know the magnitude of your achievement and so it is unnecessary for me to single out any particular group for special commendation. But there is one with us tonight, a sapper, whose clever design of the delayed action explosives that our men were able to secrete amongst the cargo during the simulated seagoing inspection, made possible the remote destruction of the whole IRA arms cache. I ask you to raise your glasses and drink a toast to the services and this brave man who attained some satisfaction for what the terrorists had inflicted on him and his colleagues."

The toast was accompanied by a roar of assent, and

across the crowded room, a man in a wheel chair drank with the aid of a straw, smiling his acknowledgment, as much as his damaged face would allow.

Manchester, UMIST Bunker

Up in Manchester a small group of nerdy men and women from the University of Manchester Institute of Science and Technology's high level cyber technology program, were enjoying an equally uninhibited celebration. They scorned the Silicon Valley addiction to burgers and Coke and the navy's pink gins were far too effete for these cyber warriors. Their exuberance was fuelled more by meat and potato pies washed down with pints of Boddington's bitter, but their victory was every bit as significant and worth celebrating as that of the sea-going commandos.

Cheltenham, GCHQ

"We have just received confirmation from our Cyber-attack team in Manchester. Mission accomplished. The cupboard is bare."

"That's great news. Thank you. I will be sure to pass it on to C immediately. After the success in Ireland this will be the icing on the cake. Please give our best to the gang up there."

London, MI6 HQ

"I have gathered you all together to thank you for your contribution to the success of this operation and to tell you what I can about events that followed on from where you left off."

"Thank you C. We are aware that the arms cache was

destroyed, but how was that done without infringing Irish sovereignty, and who did it?"

"Good question Douglas. It was a joint military operation involving multiple players. The SBS posed as Irish coast guards, boarded the cargo ship and under the pretext of inspecting the cargo, planted time delayed explosive charges amongst the munitions."

"I can appreciate their sea-faring skills, but how did they pass muster as Irish coast guard officers?"

"Firstly, they were welcomed, as the IRA had suborned some of the Irish officials, and secondly we were able to use SBS men of Irish origin to ensure authenticity. However, I must confess that they almost blew their cover by sending aboard, with the inspection party, a man with a strong Belfast accent. Fortunately this did not raise the alarm. RAF surveillance flights and SAS observation teams on the ground tracked the cargos to their destinations and allowed us to time the detonations to avoid civilian casualties."

"But what about the time delayed charges? That was a very fine piece of work, especially as the explosions occurred almost simultaneously, days later and in locations far apart. How was that done?"

"That was an especially fine piece of work done with ingenuity and deadly intent by one familiar to both of you, Eliot and Douglas. It was of course, the former mercenary who was your first informant and who suffered terrible injuries at the hands of IRA enforcers. You can be sure he feels great satisfaction and vindication at getting back at them in this way."

"We heard rumours of some involvement by GCHQ

and cyber nerds at Manchester University. What was that all about?"

"This was a particularly elegant and satisfying piece of work, in that it punished both the Russian sponsors and the Libyan suppliers of the munitions. We maintain under-cover, cyber warfare capabilities based in technology companies and universities throughout the country. With the collaboration of a GCHQ a team in their Manchester bunker, we were able to locate the Syrian Government's bank account and drain it of the funds transferred to them to pay for the arms and explosives. What a hoot. They did all that for nothing."

"What happened to the money?"

"Several notable charities and especially those looking after wounded and stressed service people,

such as Walking with the Wounded, discovered substantial anonymous donations had been lodged in their bank accounts. In particular our sapper friend and his family will want for nothing for the rest of their lives."

26
END OF THE BEGINNING

London, Foreign Office

"I wish to congratulate you gentlemen, and all your people, on the excellent execution and outcome of this operation. In one stroke you have thwarted a major terrorist plot, possibly aimed at Her Majesty, given a stern warning to Russian and Libyan Governments to respect our interests, and endeared us to our Spanish friends by helping them with their terror exposure. I am particularly pleased to have heard from the Irish Government that whilst they are very displeased by the explosions on their territory, as there was no loss of life and it is clear the IRA were responsible for bringing in the explosives, in the first place, they will ask no questions about how this was done and by whom. Also they have put the IRA on notice not to use Irish territory to plan further atrocities and that the Queen is strictly off-limits."

London, MI5 HQ

"The Foreign Secretary has asked me to convey to you both, on behalf of the government and the nation, extreme thanks for your courage and selfless service in thwarting a proposed terrorist atrocity that would have had disastrous consequences, including an incalculable loss of civilian lives. Your service is held in such high regard that you will be gazetted to receive recognition in the next honours list, but of course, because of the secret nature of your work, you will receive your awards in a private ceremony and you are constrained from revealing this to anyone else — even to your family and closest friends."

"Thank you sir. I think I can speak for Kat in saying that we are honoured to receive this award and now that the operation has been successfully completed we wonder what is next for us."

"You have done so well that I am authorised to offer both of you regular assignments with either MI5 or MI6, and I will be speaking with you separately in the next few days to discuss your career options and choices."

Manchester, Sam's Chop House

Harry Higgins pushed a pint of Guinness across the table to Ken and with uncharacteristically warm words, expressed his appreciation for what Ken had done.

"Thanks Ken for all you did for us, and for giving me this chance to farewell you and wish you all the best in your future career. You did a grand job and dare I say much better than most experienced professionals could have done."

"Thanks Harry. I can't say it was a pleasure as there were a lot of hairy moments which could have been the end of me or Kat, but I must admit that when I recall your request for my help, in this very bar, it's hard to believe that we had such a success that I could not have thought possible back then."

"I heard you turned down the offer to join on a regular basis?"

"That's right Harry. Not that I wasn't pleased and flattered to be invited, but I am too much of a loner and didn't fancy the restrictions imposed by accession to the secret world. Also, I have always nurtured the ambition to return to Australia, and for the same reasons I was advised to come home from Melbourne, your masters think it would be better for me to get lost out there and stay under the radar of those who might seek revenge. I will not be joining ASIO or ASIS, but the government has blessed my return as an Australian citizen and have indicated that they might like to use my services again in future, should a similar need arise for discreet enquiries."

"I am glad to hear that lad, as you have an aptitude for this work and it would be a pity to lose your skills and the hard-won experience you have gained. I can't do anything to match the honour you have received but in a small way I would like to share with you some professional advice and give you a practical contact that will serve you well in future.

Don't drop your guard. Terror groups like the IRA and their former Russian sponsors have long memories and their tentacles of interest reach around the globe. They will seize any opportunity for revenge and so don't forget your field craft — especially checking for followers and being aware who else is in the cafés, on tram cars, and other places you frequent. Should the worst come to the worst, please take this card and be sure to call on the person named on it. He is a former SAS trooper with significant Northern Irish undercover service and a good man to have on your side if you have to deal with the bad guys. Also, he is married to my daughter.

He is no longer in the game, but he owes me some favours and will be willing to help you, at least to the extent of helping you suss out who's who in the Australian secret and criminal world, and even fix you up with a suitable self-defence weapon. I know how strict they are down there about civilians not carrying firearms; but he can fit you up with a legal gun."

"Thanks Harry. Medals are all very well but your practical help is much more valuable and useful to me. Let me know if I can ever help you in return, and should you ever get to Melbourne, it's my shout."

Manchester, Midland Hotel

Ken really enjoyed visiting the Midland, especially for the all-in breakfast that left out nothing desired by a connoisseur. It was a special pleasure to be eating in the grand dining room, where Rolls and Royce had met and agreed to start a motor car company. As usual, Kat wore an unassuming, simple number that accentuated her tan and the fitness of her lithe body.

"Hi Kat. Thanks for coming all the way up from London to see me off. You are just in time, as I fly out to Melbourne tomorrow."

"G'day, Ken. I wouldn't have missed it for quids, and the Midland puts on a good spread."

"So, you have elected to stay in the game."

"Yes, I have. Unlike you, I always wanted to be a professional and after what I have been through to win acceptance, I am loath to give all that away. Besides, I would miss the adrenalin rush in any other occupation I am qualified for, and all my mates in Sydney have either married or moved on. What are you going to do back there?"

"I couldn't go back to the routine of HR work as, like you, I have developed a taste for the unexpected and the challenge of the chase. A friend has offered me a desk and chair in his Lygon Street consulting office in Carlton, and unless I die of excess pasta and great coffee, I am sure work will come my way. Special Branch has agreed to keep an eye out for anyone seeking to do me any harm and I may pick up the odd contract job for them."

They had much to reminisce about, especially the deadly situations they had faced and won through. They agreed to stay in touch and Kat promised to call him when she intended returning to Australia. It was late when they parted — Kat for her room in the hotel and Ken to his brother's house.

"You will always be special to me Kat. Be sure to keep in touch."

"Same here Ken. See you on Lygon or at the Melbourne Cup."

Melbourne, on Lygon Street

Lygon Street was a great place to work. Ken spent little time in the small but functional office he had leased from his friend, and for the first few days since his return, he held court with friends and contacts under the sun umbrellas outside various Italian cafés and bars. His office block was across the street from Borsari, the cycling champion's shop, close to the Grattan Street corner, and in the centre of the 'eating out' action.

Richmond had transformed itself from industrial slum to inner city 'place to be' for the bright young lawyers, accountants and IT specialists working in the city. Having made killings from selling their Balwyn mansions to wealthy Chinese, age-defying, empty-nesters who had invested in slick inner-city apartments and town houses, took to sporting their stylishly torn jeans and Port Douglas T-shirts outside numerous outdoor cafes. Ken felt at home there too, and had settled in a bright, two-bedroom, first-floor-apartment at the top of Richmond Hill, where nineteenth-century business moguls built their mansions — well above their noisome, factories and workers' shanty-towns.

For the first few weeks he had busied himself with 'rats and mice' consulting jobs for his friend until, one spring evening, he called in at the Grand on Burnley Street to refresh himself with a pint of cool dark ale and tuck into the best Parma and chips in Melbourne. He was seated in the beer garden with his back to the wall of the neighbouring Greek Orthodox Church, relaxed but fully aware of the regulars around him and any new arrivals coming his way. He had dipped his head to take in a mouthful of food when a shadow fell across his table and an all too familiar voice from the past greeted him.

"G'day, Ken. Have another dark on me."

"Hi George. I expected to see you again, but not so soon after my return. What do you want from me this time?"

"First of all, welcome back. Glad to see you here where

you belong. Yes, we want something from you, but it is as much in your interest as ours."

"Thanks. It's good to be back, but what's this about my interest in what you are about to propose?"

"We received word from London that an IRA hit squad is on the way, traveling as supporters of a visiting hurling team. Usually, we would turn them back but MI6 want us to let them in and prepare an entrapment when they reveal their target."

"Why should this be of special interest to me?"

"Intelligence indicates that they are the same crew that tortured and crippled your English informant and that they are seeking revenge for the arms shipment fiasco."

"Unless they are targeting me, I can't see what I can add to your ability to deal with them."

"They are not after you, and their target has been selected by that renegade KGB unit which lost such face due to the destruction of the munitions and the loss of money they had invested in the operation. Kat is coming home for a family visit, and news of her plans has been picked up by the opposition."

"She must be stopped and put under protection."

"It's not as simple as that Ken. This is a deliberate plan to flush out the IRA, and Kat has volunteered to be the bait. But only on condition that you are part of the back-up team, as she trusts you more than anyone to keep her safe."

"But that's madness. They are ruthless and brutal, and you know that we cannot guarantee to protect her at all times."

"You are quit right, but London wants these guys taken

out for good and she is insistent that she will be the lure. They finally worked out who the mysterious Australian woman is that ruined their plans, and they are so keen to settle the score they have sent their most experienced hit squad to execute her. We have a day or two yet before we need to act, so I guess you will want to think this over and let me know whether you want to be in on it."

"Mate! This is Kat's life we are talking about. I don't need to think about it. I am most definitely in."

"Good on yer Ken. I knew you would join us. I will pick you up early tomorrow morning and take you to a strategy meeting at our headquarters in town."

Richmond, The Four Nations Hotel

Later that evening, Ken met up with Harry's son-in-law at the Four Nations Hotel. Its snug bar and generally well-warn appearance did not attract the younger push and was usually quiet on a week night. It was an ideal place for a discreet meeting.

"Hi Pete, what will you have?"

"It's my shout Ken. I think you like that dark stuff."

They took their drinks to a corner table away from the cluster of people by the fire and Ken wasted no time in getting to the point of the meeting.

"Harry said that if I was in need, you could help me get tooled up without my having to go via the authorities. That time has come and I need an automatic hand gun with superior stopping power."

"If Harry vouches for you, it's OK with me, and I can help you, but I would appreciate your assurance that you don't intend to use it for anything criminal."

"What I want it for is legal, but as it is covered by the Official Secrets Act, I can't reveal any detail other than to say it is the same sort of anti-terrorist work that Harry is involved in."

"That's good enough for me Ken. I appreciate your need to keep shtum, but I will assume that those IRA bastards are involved, and to go up against them I will fix you up with the latest Glock automatic that is favoured by Special-Forces units on hostage release missions. It's totally reliable, quick firing and deadly at close range. When do you need it?"

"I know I am being unreasonable, but ASAP as I will be briefed tomorrow morning and the action could follow on before the week is out."

"No sweat Ken. Through being in the British SAS I have some mates from the Australian regiment and finding a weapon for such a good cause will not be a problem. Tell me where you will be over the next few days and I will get it to you with a good supply of ammo. I guess you know how to use one?"

"For sure! They were standard issue for UK agents and I became familiar with one during my training."

"I don't want you to betray any confidences, but if ASIO, and especially a bloke called George is involved, remember me to him and tell him that if he needs any 'off-establishment' help, me and my mates would welcome a crack at the paddies. I can guarantee competence and confidentiality and we come reasonably cheap."

"Thanks Pete. I will be sure to put a word in for you."

27
CHERCHEZ LA FEMME!

Melbourne, MCG

"George, why have you chosen the footy match at the MCG for the show down?"

"Kat will be in a corporate box, so any attempt on her will not risk harming any of the public. You will be with her, and Pete will be a guest, along with a few of his former SAS mates. As we didn't want our plans to leak, the waiters will be unaware of what's going on, and as the killers will have local help, putting our people in could have given the game away.

The venue will appeal to the gunmen as they will have contacts in the football fraternity, and it will allow us to deploy extra police and a helicopter without raising suspicions. Also, they will believe they can make their escape by mingling with the home-going crowd."

Game day

"The match was a local derby involving traditional foes and had drawn a crowd in excess of eighty-thousand. The assailants had been spotted entering the ground, but although the close fought game was coming to its end they had made no move. Kat needed to go to the toilet and one of the female catering staff offered to accompany her and show her where it was.

The excitement of the finish, which resulted in a draw, distracted the security team, and it was only when the full-time siren sounded and she had not returned, that Ken raised the alarm. He became even more anxious when there was no further sign of the waitress, and the regulars told him she was a temp they had not worked with before. They had not thought to include a female agent in their team and George's people had only vetted the regular catering staff.

There was no sign of her in the ladies' room, and the lack of any evidence of a struggle and bloodshed gave them some comfort and hope that she was alive. The hue and cry was general but ineffective. There was no sign of her or of her captors. Police searched all the nooks and crannies of the ground, crowds were funnelled through check points and their helicopter swept over surrounding suburbs searching for any sighting.

It was half an hour after she had gone missing that a rather sheepish police inspector reported that one vehicle had left the ground, just before the siren. It was an ambulance carrying a woman who had suffered a heart attack and was accompanied by a doctor with an Irish accent. Two of his motor cyclists had provided an escort to get them through the traffic and ensure they got away un-hindered by snarl-ups. As he reported his radio bleeped and he received news that the patrolmen had been found in Punt Road, shot but not fatally wounded. There was no sign of the ambulance.

Melbourne, ASIO HQ

While a state-wide manhunt for the terrorists continued, Ken and his colleagues met at ASIO headquarters to figure out their next move.

"They certainly outsmarted us, and our failure to vet the catering staff more fully was our Achilles heel."

"You are right George, but going over our past errors will not save Kat which must be our key concern."

"Sorry Ken, that was a bit insensitive of me. Looking on the brighter side, our experts say that the longer the search fails to find her suggests that she is more valuable to her kidnappers alive than dead. The dilemma is: do we wait to hear from them and their demands, or is there anything we can do in the meanwhile, other than conduct a thorough search?"

"You are right George. We must rely on the professionalism of our searchers, but as Kat and I learned in Europe, sometimes, unorthodox thinking and action comes up with an answer before the experts can. We need to pull together our volunteer team of locals and ask what we would do in the kidnappers' shoes. Pete and his boys could be really helpful here."

Melbourne, RSL Club conference room

"Thanks to you all for agreeing to help us and for arranging this venue, away from the media glare. It's vital that we keep the opposition guessing about what we are doing, in addition to the public search for Kat. What are your initial thoughts, Pete?"

"These guys are professionals and probably have the backing of a foreign intelligence agency with resources here in Melbourne. Despite this, I don't think they could have got far away with her before we closed down the obvious escape routes. The ambulance would have been too obvious, all roads and rail outlets were tightly screened, and even a helicopter would not have escaped the attention of the Police Air Wing and flight controllers at Tullamarine. So they can't be far away, and all we can rely on is the hope they will make a mistake and reveal their hideaway to an alert member of the public.

Those of us here with Northern Ireland experience agree with you George, that as they would want to make an example of her, it is unlikely they would execute and dispose of her without maximum publicity. So, no news is good news. Also, it suggests they may want more from this than just revenge on Kat — perhaps release of some of their convicted 'soldiers.'"

"Yes, we must remember that the Russians will have an interest in this, and assuming they have no appetite for starting a tit-for-tat war at this time, the recovery of their lost finances might satisfy them sufficiently to keep the terror merchants in check. How about you Ken. What do you make of our options?"

"My prime concern is for Kat. Whilst they might not have killed her yet, I fear what they might do to her before we can either find her or do a deal. I suggest our best bet is to use our back channel connections with the Russians' new security service, the FSB, to confirm this is being sponsored by a renegade wing of the old KGB, and to dangle the possibility of a monetary solution in return for Kat's release."

"I think that's our best option and I will make the

suggestion to my seniors in the secret service that they make contact with their Russian counterparts without delay. In the meanwhile, you guys should continue to use your local knowledge and contacts to find out where they might be holding her."

"Thanks George. I will continue to work with Pete and the boys to see if we can find a lead to them."

28
JOURNEY'S END

Canberra, ASIO HQ

The demand came in via a recorded voice message, and in true IRA style was validated by the inclusion of a recognised IRA code. Their request was simple — repayment of the money stolen from the Libyan bank account. But the method of delivery was not. The payment was to come in the form of gold bars. The hand-over of the gold in exchange for Kat was to take place in international waters off the North-West coast of Australia, where a Russian ship would accept the cargo, and at its signal, Kat would be released in Melbourne.

This proposal was accepted and it was agreed that the Royal Australian Navy would load the gold in Fremantle and sail it north along the coast to the proposed rendezvous. When the cargo had been authenticated by the Russian ship's captain, Kat would be released in Melbourne's Southern Cross Station, during either the morning or evening rush hours, on the appointed day. Only one person was to receive her, and as they knew him, they insisted that Ken Eliot should be that person.

"The gold delivery will be a routine task for the navy, and as long as the sea is calm the armed patrol boat and aerial reconnaissance will ensure the Russians keep their side of the bargain, before allowing them to sail off with the gold. The shallow draft of the patrol boat enables it to operate in coastal waters should that be necessary. What worries me, Minister, is exposing Ken along with Kat to the mercies of the IRA assassins in a crowded railway station, especially as construction on the new station is starting, which will add to congestion and provide even more places for them to hide."

"I understand your concern DG, but just as we rely on the professionalism of the navy, you will have to trust your people to handle the Melbourne hand-over without any slip up. They outsmarted you once and I am sure that will not happen again."

"I assure you that there will be no underestimate on this occasion."

St Petersburg, former KGB HQ

"We are in serious trouble Piotr. I have just come from that bastard new Prime Minister, Putin. He's a hard-arse former KGB man who served in Germany and he left me in no doubt that the KGB was finished and that we must cease our operations. But he put a proposition to me that, if we could recover from the recent embarrassment of the IRA fiasco and loss of money, there would be a chance to maintain my rank in the new Federal Security Service — the FSB. So, we had better not allow the IRA to stuff-up in Australia."

"If your plan to recover the money stolen from the Libyans goes to plan, he is bound to be pleased."

"Yes. He will be even more pleased if we teach MI6 a

lesson by eliminating the two British agents who caused us so much trouble, especially the man who killed our agent and broke the anti-Croat operation a few years back."

Richmond, All Nations Hotel

"You wanted to see me Pete?"

"Sure do Ken. We have a breakthrough. One of my SAS mates who comes from Carrickfergus near Belfast, drinks in an Irish pub in Footscray, and the other night he overheard a drunken local shooting his mouth off about IRA men playing hurly in Melbourne. That's all he heard before the drunk's mates bundled him out."

"That's all you got?"

"No, or I wouldn't be bothering you now. It so happens that the guy is a bit of a playboy locally and my wife told me his wife is a notably devout attendee at St Ignatius on Richmond Hill. We caught up with him whilst he was enjoying an early pint here and put it to him that if he didn't tell us more about the location of these Fenians, his wife might get chapter and verse about his womanising with Asian girls in Footscray. He was terrified of IRA retribution, but his fear of his wife and risk of losing her frightened him even more and he coughed.

"What did he tell you?"

"They are shacked up with an Irish landlady in Collingwood, and they make a big thing of learning to sail on Albert Park Lake. I had one of my mates follow them and sure enough they go to an old boat house on the lake, but they don't do any sailing. They spend all the time there in the boat house and bring daily supplies of food from a local 7-Eleven, including women's necessities. He managed to get close up to the building after dusk and he's certain he could hear a woman crying. Seems that one man stays with her all the time and they operate a shift system in keeping her under guard."

"He took a brave risk. I hope he wasn't spotted."

"He is a dab hand at working under cover. In Belfast during the troubles he drove a dry cleaning van through the Catholic areas collecting garments and having them checked for explosives' traces before they were cleaned and returned. If he had been tagged as an SAS trooper his life would have been short-lived. He is very good at going unseen."

"Thank you Pete. You and your men have probably saved her life."

"No problem Ken. We still have some scores to settle with those gentlemen and if you would like some unofficial, deniable help in taking them out, we would be happy to oblige."

"Thanks mate. I certainly will if I can. I must not get the security services completely offside, but George and I have worked together under the official radar before, and I am sure he will come to the party and give us the OK to go in."

Melbourne, Albert Park Lakeside

The plan to use outsiders to take on the assassins was approved with some reluctance, but the pedigree of Pete and his comrades swayed the balance in their favour, and the deniability factor was equally appealing to the spooks. The secrecy and timing of their action was critical.

The gold-bearing boat was well on its way north and nothing should be done to spook the Russians. At the same time, it was vital to establish whether there were other IRA men in town or local sympathisers who might be delegated to join in the delivery of Kat to the station. On the day before the navy was scheduled to make the rendezvous, Ken got the green light to go.

Ken, Pete and three of the ex-SAS men were ready to take on the men in the boat house, as soon as the sun went down. They had blackened their faces, covered their heads with balaclavas and all wore dark boiler suits. Pete and his mates had somehow acquired silenced, Heckler and Koch KP5 sub machine guns, and Ken carried both his Glock automatic and hunter's crossbow. The area around the boathouse was unlit and there appeared to be no watchers, and even dog walkers had gone home at dark-fall.

Ken stood back and left first entry to the professionals. At a nod from Pete, a trooper kicked the unsubstantial door in and the others tossed in flash grenades to temporarily blind the occupants. The groaning and thrashing around of those inside confirmed their confusion and disability, and no give-away sound had accompanied the brief flash of blinding light. He was about to follow them in when he heard the loud thud of running feet as a man darted from the shadows by the hut and raced away.

He ran for his life, and until the thrumming sound stopped and the relentlessly pursuing bolt pierced his neck, severing his windpipe, he thought he had made it. Ken ensured he was beyond saving and folding away his crossbow, returned to join the others. He was pleased to see the two remaining IRA men lying on the floor, gagged and bound with plastic ties and to his relief Kat was receiving help to restore circulation to her unbound arms and legs. But then, to his horror, he saw her ravaged right hand which was missing the three finger nails that lay in a bloody pool in a tin bowl by her chair. The array of pincers, saws, power drill and blow torch, foretold what further horrors she might have suffered, but for their timely arrival.

Rushing to her side, he enveloped her in his arms and whispered in her ear: "Oh sweetheart. I am so sorry that we fucked up and let this happen to you. Don't say anything. Just, lean on me. Medics are on the way and we will soon have your hand seen to."

One of the boys produced a syringe from his combat survival kit and injected her with sufficient pain killer and tranquiliser to still her shaking and put her to sleep.

George burst through the door backed by a team of heavily armed agents.

"Great work you blokes. The local cops have been distracted, but we need to get Kat away in the medivac vehicle outside, and be far from here before they and the media are alerted to the disturbance. We have collected the body outside and my men will bring the prisoners and clear up any obvious signs of what happened here."

Melbourne, ASIO safe house

Ken wasn't sure where they were, but the sound of waves lapping on a shore placed the safe house somewhere by the bay. He was boiling with anger at what the terrorists had done to Kat and their Oldham informer friend, and though not addicted to sadistic violence, he dearly wanted to hurt the captives. But George kept him away from them and only allowed him to observe Pete's boys, through the one-way viewing, glass wall, as they began to interrogate the two men.

At first he was impatient with their seemingly slow approach, but as time went on he began to appreciate the subtlety of their methods. First the men had been kept for hours in separate, confined, starkly-lit and sound-proofed cells, without food or water. Then came a period of questioning which seemed to further erode their composure. The Northern Irishmen knew what to say to confuse and frighten these otherwise hard-boiled, southern killers. After this, it was back to the cells and finally the interview room. But this time an array of wicked instruments were strewn on a bloody towel on a side table, and a recording of the occasional scream of someone supposedly in extreme pain, echoed in from along the corridor outside. When the questioning stopped, the weakest of the pair was strapped to the chair, and Pete pulled on gauntlets and with a lit blow torch, waved it over the man's exposed genitals.

A combination of the reflected heat singeing his pubic hair and his imagination broke him, and with a shriek of promised compliance he began to tell all, between deep sighs and body-wracking sobs.

Both men told the same story, and George and Ken were relieved to hear that only they and their dead comrade, were involved in the kidnapping of Kat. They gave up the code that was to indicate to the Russians that all was well at this end, and that they had disposed of both

Kat and Ken at Southern Cross Station. Now it was down to the Navy to seal the bargain.

**North West Australia,
somewhere off the Kimberley coast**

The captain of the Australian patrol boat confirmed receipt of the signal advising of Kat's safe release.

"Signaller, send the following message to our Russian friends on that over-large cargo ship out there:

'Good evening Captain. I am afraid to advise you that there will be no transfer of cargo today, as the price of gold in Australia has been inflated beyond the value of what you are able to offer in exchange.'"

The Russian ship's signaller requested a repeat of the message to ensure they had understood it properly. After that there was a prolonged period of silence and no discernible movement on the Russian vessel and all its lights were extinguished. It was assumed that they had been shocked by the unexpectedly negative message and that they were taking time to contact their government for further orders. When their reply came it was far from friendly:

'You have broken the agreement made between our countries and we regret to advise you that if you are unable to complete your part of the bargain by transferring the gold, we shall be forced to take hostile action against you.'

This was followed by the total illumination of the Russian ship, revealing that far from being an innocent, unarmed cargo boat, it was a camouflaged fighting vessel, whose array of weaponry made it more than capable of sinking the patrol boat.

"Well! Well! I'll be damned!" murmured the Australian captain. "The Admiral was right to suspect this subterfuge. First, send the coded flash message and then transmit the following to the Russian:

'*Message received and understood. We confirm that we are still unable to meet your terms, but before you commence hostile actions towards us, I suggest you look out to the North West and confirm whether what you see might change your intentions.*'"

At that moment a shaft of light illuminated a patch of sea North West of the Russians. What they saw seemed to have changed their minds as the war ship got under way, turned off all but its navigation lights and sailed, at increasing speed, away from the patrol boat whose captain smiled as he sent off a final signal:

'*Intruder departed. Thanks for your assistance.*'

The recipient of this message rapped out new orders and the huge threatening mass of the Royal Australian Navy's Collins Class submarine switched off its deck lights, closed its torpedo tubes and submerged to sail for home.

Canberra, ASIO HQ

"Excellent outcome, George — IRA warned off by the Irish and British governments, KGB renegades shut down by an embarrassed Putin, and no doubt the responsible General is rueing his folly in a gulag, far removed from St Petersburg. You were right about Ken Eliot and the remarkable Kat Douglas, they are very resourceful and you should keep your eye on Ken, now that he has settled back in Melbourne. I understand he is setting himself up in Carlton as some sort of security consultant. We could have use for his talents again in future should a similar delicate situation arise."

"Yes Minister. I agree and thank you also for endorsing my proposal for the payment of an ex-gratia reward to those splendid former SAS blokes. They did a great job and might be useful too if and when we need some deniable, 'off the books' assistance."

Carlton, il Vicolo Ristorante

"How are you going Kat? I must say that surgeon did a great job on your hand. Those new painted nails look beautifully natural."

"Sharp enough to see through your flattery Ken, and fit enough to leave a memento of my new steel nails, carved in that handsome cheek of yours, if you don't go easy on the soft soap."

"Have another glass of this excellent Shiraz and tell me what you intend doing now."

"Back to London. I am still contracted to work with MI5 and there are still a few minor loose ends associated with what happened here that I have agreed to clear up. How about you?"

"I'm staying here. I really like Melbourne, especially the inner city life, and it certainly justifies its world's most liveable city reputation. I have finally realised that I am no longer the accidental Englishman helping governments out of a mess.

What we have achieved in these past few years has confirmed that I have some talent for this work, and though I have no psychotic leanings, I have become somewhat hardened to the necessary violence, when public safety is the aim."

"George and his masters think very highly of you. Why don't you join ASIO or ASIS?"

"Since leaving corporate life I have realised that I am not a joiner and I will be happier and more successful working on my own, taking on only the most interesting assignments and on completion, riding off to another town, seeking another sheriff who needs the help of a temporary deputy."

"Sounds good and it's really you. But do be careful. Now that I have you as the best and most trusted friend in my life, I don't want to lose you."

"Thanks Kat. I feel the same about you, and you must promise to call me when you are down this way again. Don't worry about me. George will keep an eye out for me. The Federal Police and the State blokes are aware of me, and then through my mate Pete I have my own private, and oh so deadly, Special Forces."

"Make sure they do, and if I hear you are taking too many wild risks, I will come back and haunt you."

"Here's to us and what the future brings. Cheers!"

ABOUT THE AUTHOR

Barry Smith was born in England and educated in Manchester and at Cambridge University, where he read history. Australia has been home for over 50 years and he lives in marvellous Melbourne, where he is now living his dream of being a published writer.

Most of Barry's career has been in HR management and for 20 years before retirement he ran his own consulting business, focusing on turning around toxic management teams. Since retiring he has completed a doctorate focused on *"How I want to live and work in what's left of my life"* and over the past 10 years he has pursued dreams emanating from that—such as, crossing Siberia, touring Moorish Spain, finding his Manchester Regiment, Grandad's grave at Gallipoli, crossing USA by train and camp touring around Australia, carrying out research for and selling his Kimberley Trilogy of historical novels, in pubs and on outdoor markets from Cooktown to Broome and back.

Books about his travels—*Wordspinner's Way, My Russian Dreamroad, My Spanish Dreamroad, My American Dreamrailroad* —recount and illustrate with photographs and 'Brysonesque' commentary, Barry's travels around Australia, selling books in pubs and on markets, living in St Petersburg and crossing Siberia, touring Moorish

Andalusia and railroading across the USA from sea to shining sea and back. These can be ordered from Blurb at au.blurb.com.

You can follow Barry's further musings and adventures on his website blog at barrysmithwordspinner.com or on Facebook at facebook.com/barrysmithwordspinner.

Where to get the books

Paperbacks and eBooks can be ordered online
from Amazon and from any major bookstore.

THE KIMBERLEY TRILOGY
Book 1

FOR FREEDOM'S CAUSE

For Freedom's Cause is a historical, romantic thriller set in England and Australia between the world wars. It follows the adventures and growing relationship between a working class English Army Officer, from Manchester — Dan Bevan — and a Melbourne barrister, serving with the Australian Light Horse — Charlie Elliott — who met, by chance, during the First World War and the strong women in their lives.

Having survived several of the major battles, both men are so disillusioned with the homes and occupations they return to, that Dan volunteers to suppress the republican rebellion in Ireland and Charlie joins an underground army to stand-up against mob riots in Melbourne. Despite their contrasting social origins and differing views on what form of government is best for preserving freedom and maintaining civil order, they become firm friends and when Dan is targeted by vengeful IRA assassins, he accepts Charlie's invitation to escape to Australia where he intends settling down peacefully in Melbourne, with the love of his life who unknown to him has born him a son.

When IRA gunmen pursue him from Melbourne to Perth he is forced to flee to a cattle station in the Kimberley where, finally reunited with his wife and son, he confronts his nemesis in that vast and mystical wilderness.

THE KIMBERLEY TRILOGY
Book 2

BATTLE FOR THE NORTH

Battle for the North reunites the heroes and heroines of *For Freedom's Cause* — Dan, Charlie, Elspeth Liza and Alice, in frustrating Japanese espionage plots and raids into northern Australia during World War 2. The action takes place in the Kimberley wilderness and celebrates the daring and heroism of mounted North Australian Observer Unit patrols, nicknamed the 'Nackeroos' or 'Curtin's Cowboys.'

Following on the bombing of Darwin and Broome, Japanese marine commandos land on the Kimberley coast to establish a foothold and deny the US and Australian Navies a secure re-fuelling and supply base. In the absence of Australia's regular forces in the Middle East and Singapore, all that stands between them and success is Dan Bevan's and Charlie Elliott's part-time observer patrols, which battle a Japanese special forces unit from Broome to their Kalumburu base and join the fight to push the enemy back into the sea.

Whilst Dan and Charlie conduct their guerrilla campaign in the bush, their wives and Lady Elspeth interrupt their war work in Darwin to hunt down a murderous Spy.

THE KIMBERLEY TRILOGY
Book 3

KIMBERLEY KILL

Kimberley Kill is the final novel in the trilogy. An international, religious war has broken out across the Middle East between Sunni and Shia Islamic sects, cutting off all energy supplies from that region. Frustrated by its inability to acquire sufficient energy to power its ever expanding economy, China has invaded Russia, annexing the Siberian oil and gas fields and precipitating World War 3. Cyber warfare has neutralised global defence communications creating a US-China stand-off and the only remaining operational satellite communication base in the Kimberley is threatened by invading Indonesian, special-forces. All that stands in their way is a small Norforce patrol backed by an Aboriginal tribe, whose female leader is intent on avenging the murder of her father, their Elder, and the desecration of their Wandjina guardian. Three strong minded and determined people — the devout Moslem leader of the Indonesian Kopassus force, the MIT trained daughter of an assassinated Aboriginal elder and the middle-aged, former SAS, gas platform engineer and part-time leader of the Norforce patrol — strive to contest and impose their conflicting beliefs and loyalties when they compete and clash in a hunt to the death across the harsh but beautiful Kimberley wilderness.

VICTORIA'S TWINS

The rise of Manchester and Melbourne
*Tales of fighting for freedoms,
fortunes and football*

This is a rich and dramatic historical novel that experiences the flowering of Manchester and Melbourne, two of the most significant cities of Queen Victoria's Empire, as they emerged and flourished during the turbulent years of the 19th and early 20th centuries.

Both gave birth to world famous, liberal leaning newspapers, *The Manchester Guardian* and *The Melbourne Age*, which referee the game through the astutely, forensic eyes of their most illustrious and campaigning editors, C.P. Scott and David Syme, but, who still can't help taking sides and entering the play.

It is in two parts.

Firstly, The Beginning Years, from 1854 to the start of WWI, follows the life and adventures of a former *Manchester Guardian* compositor who migrates to Melbourne in time to join *The Age*, as it reports the beginning of the Eureka rebellion and starts to comment on and shape the colony's and Australia's turbulent path to state and nationhood. With the constant oversight of Scott and Syme drawing out the similarities with Manchester's complementary fight for civil and political liberties and economic power.

Secondly, The Later Years relates experiences and escapades of a contemporary Manchester migrant, fleeing the dead hand of British socialism in the sixties only to land in the thick of Gough Whitlam's Prime Ministership and the gradual awakening of Melbourne from its prudish and censorial post war manacles to become the exciting cultural melting pot, and social, sporting and culinary pace-setter for Australia, that it is today.

As at many times in their histories, *The Guardian* and *The Age* are in serious, if not terminal, economic trouble, but their great powerhouse cities thrive and grow in the 21st century as never before.

COMING SOON

DRAGON'S BREATH

Blackmail, sabotage and murder shatter the calm of an Australian bush town: unrelated acts of evil or a plot to undermine the community and take it over?

A routine job for Ken Eliot threatens his life and growing evidence of outside influence drives him back into ASIO's ranks, re-uniting him with the deceptive and deadly Kat Douglas.

Family fiefdoms, fanaticism, foreign plots and football form the strands of this web of intrigue. Ken will fight for his life with Kat guarding his back. Will they again expose and overcome the dark forces threatening the life and freedoms of Australia itself?

This exciting sequel to *Terror Trails* will be available early in 2018.